THE CURSE OF WHITEHALL MANOR

A GOTHIC HORROR NOVEL

TOWRY
BOOK TWO

L.V. PIRES

PANGRAM PUBLISHING

CONTENTS

PROLOGUE

"Do you want to tell us what happened?" the investigator asked.

I rocked back and forth. My hands slid through my greasy hair. I could still smell the blood on me. A dull ache pulsed in my womb. "I need a doctor," I said.

"You'll get one. Sooner than you know," the woman across from me said. "Now, how about you tell me your version of things."

"I've told you," I hissed. "I've told you a hundred times."

"Tell us again," the man said.

My palms pressed against my temples. "The curse."

"I don't believe in curses," he said, narrowing his gaze. "I do believe in murderers though." He turned to the woman and whispered something.

My eyes widened. "Y-you won't put me in the asylum." Tears flooded my red-strained eyes. "You can't put me away." I clasped my hands and rocked again. "You can't do this to me. I must return to Whitehall Manor. I must go back."

The investigator turned a cold eye to me and said, "You want to go back?"

I had chewed my lips raw. The taste of blood lingered on my tongue. "I'll tell you whatever you want to know. I want someone to believe me."

The woman leaned closer. The hard lines around her eyes relaxed. Her voice cut the tension in the room. "I'll believe you," she said. "Tell us the truth, Anne. Your version of it."

"M-my version?"

She nodded.

I swallowed and took a breath. "The bones. It all started when I found the bones."

PART ONE
MARCH

CHAPTER
ONE

The chill of early spring winds rustled through my hair as I bent to touch the twisted bones buried ten inches beneath the roots of my favorite marigold. I stepped back and tightened my grip on the gardening spade. My heart thudded in my chest. What poked out from underground was undeniably bones, small, gray, and fragile, connected through an intricate maze of rib cage and spine.

It took several minutes but finally, I had unearthed what I could from the dirt. Two bowed femurs connected to the fragments of hip bone lay before me. I tore off my gloves and continued to dig with my fingertips until the whole skeleton was exposed. My stomach turned.

Gazing back at me were the empty eye sockets of a child. The hollowed black orbs now filled with dirt sent a wave of dread through me. The skull, larger than the body, looked alien-like. I leaned closer to touch the cheekbone when suddenly a voice called out.

"Anne, are you alright?"

Terran stood feet away from me at the edge of the

Marigold Garden. His dark brows were drawn together. My expression must have alarmed him. He rushed to my side. His eyes trailed to the recently thawed ground and widened when they fell on the small bones.

"They're human," I said.

He lowered to his knees to examine them more closely. "I've worked every inch of this garden. How did they get here?"

"I don't know." I shuddered.

He stood and wrapped his warm arms around me.

I pressed my cheek to his. The stubble of his beard scratched my soft skin. I pulled back and searched his deep blue eyes for a moment of serenity. If I could find it, it would be with him. His soft lips brushed against mine. He cradled my cheek. In his strong hands, the fear melted. I held him. The earthy scent that clung to his shirt grounded me.

"Don't worry," he said. "I'll take care of this. Let's get you back to the house."

I hesitated. I could handle this without returning to the house, but Terran's grip on my hand was firm and the soothing tone of his voice made me relent. I wanted to be taken care of. I'd spent a lifetime never letting anyone get near me. I let him guide me from the Marigold Garden, through the pathways of the boxwood maze, past the wide expanse of green manicured lawns to the driveway that led back to the main house.

"Try not to think about what you saw," he said.

It was impossible to erase from my mind what I had dug up. Just as everything finally felt settled and the horror of my father's death began to dissipate. Now this.

"It was a child—a baby," I said to Terran, gripping his hand tighter.

"We don't know that. It could be animal bones."

"No." I shook my head. "I know it was a baby. I saw the skull. It was deformed, but the skull ... was human."

"I'll call Detective Richards to come take a look."

Not again. Not more police investigations. No more scouring Whitehall Manor for bodies. No more questions. Detective Richards had already been all over the property only a few months ago, searching every inch for Maura Wells' body and finally discovering it near the staff's entrance. How could he not find this?

We got back to the house. Inside, the warm smells from the kitchen wafted toward me, freshly baked bread and the chef's famous spiced tea with cinnamon and nutmeg served at every breakfast, but instead of excitement, I felt a wave of nausea hit me.

Terran led me to the fire burning strong in the stone hearth. The ten-foot opening held a huge grate piled with wood. It was the heart of Whitehall Manor. It sent warmth to every room when the central heating was turned off. The feat of engineering still amazed me. I sat down on the cushioned chair, warming my hands by the flames.

"My stomach isn't right," I said to him.

"Let me get you something warm to drink."

"Yes, that might help."

He turned and rushed through the west wing door to the kitchen.

My cheeks felt flushed near the warmth of the fire. I couldn't forget what I'd seen, the image of the bones burned into my every thought. I gazed into the fire feeling transported to the memory of sitting in this spot in the late autumn of the previous year.

So much had happened in that time. I touched my cheek thinking back to how the haunting of Whitehall

Manor had taken a toll on me. Seeing my mother's dead body and then finding my father locked in the attic had been too much to bear. If not for Terran and the windfall of the inheritance, I didn't know if I could go on. But I was a Towry, stubborn and determined. Perhaps to a fault. I shifted from the heat and went to the nearby bathroom. After running the cold water on a washcloth, I pressed it to my face.

They say what you see in the mirror reflects your inner emotions. In the bathroom mirror, my reflection showed a hazy pink glow in my cheeks while faint red lines twisted through the whites of my eyes. I was thirty-four now and looked more like the lady of the manor than a year ago when I had nothing to my name. My hair was twisted into a tight knot on top of my head. Small pearl earrings, normally reserved for dinner, seemed to make it into my ears every morning as if by routine.

I had even started to dress the part. Even though I favored simple jeans and a t-shirt, every so often I rummaged through my mother's closet and found a long dress to slip into or a pair of her elegant heels. I couldn't part with her clothing or other items that reminded me of her. A simple dab of her lilac perfume on my wrists or a touch of her makeup brush to my cheeks, made me feel more connected to her than any of her journal entries. I missed her so much. The dull ache lived in me.

I examined my eyes to see their almond shape and amber speckles that my mother once said reminded her of burning embers. I ran a finger across my thin nose and smoothed my high brows. I had so much of Father's face, too, a strong jawline and high forehead. I loosened my hair tie and pulled out my long dark hair. It fell to my shoulders, the light perfumed scent of the previous evening's shampoo lingered in the air. There was one thing about me that was different for sure. I felt the growing bump at my waist. It had been three months and I knew without a doubt the changes that were happening to me meant I was pregnant.

"Ms. Towry," the housekeeper's voice echoed from the other side of the door. "Are you okay?"

"Yes," I said, stepping from the bathroom. "Just a scare." I took the fragile teacup from her hands. It rattled in my hands as I sipped the warm liquid. Penelope's mint tea coated my stomach and brought almost instant relief to my aches. I didn't know how I'd ever survive without her help.

"Please, sit down," Penelope said, guiding me back toward the fire.

"I'll be fine," I said. "Did you see Terran?"

"Yes, I spoke to him. He's on the phone with the police department now."

I put the teacup on the side table and sighed. "Not the best of circumstances when the contractor is supposed to begin work on the upper rooms today."

Penelope patted my arm. There was something so kind in her angel-blue eyes. She had a natural proclivity for helping others and made the perfect housekeeper.

"Can I have the chef make you some toast?" she asked.

"Yes, please," I said, watching her as she hurried back to the kitchen.

We had made it through the harshest of the winter season. January and February were brutally frigid. The snow that drifted down from the sky like a blanket in December turned to ice and rain at the beginning of the year that slowed the progress on Whitehall Manor's renovations, but enough had been done to pull the two-hundred-year-old home from the depths of its decay to the beautiful and stately bayside home that it once was with some modern touches.

The sitting room had hardly needed the amount of work that most of the rest of the house needed. Only the windows needed to be replaced. The whole room had been repainted and the floors sanded to perfection. The filth that had been left behind from years of neglect and hoarding had been washed clean. New plumbing, electricity, and heat made the home livable. The antique rugs had been cleaned and restored to their rightful places. The crackle of wood in the fire brought back memories of sitting here in this spot while the ghosts of the past swirled around me whispering thoughts during the day and screaming cries of terror at night.

Those horrible memories were a thing of the past. Once Maura Wells' body had been found and removed from the property, Whitehall Manor had become a calm and quiet sanctuary.

"Here you go, Ms. Towry," Penelope said as she returned to the room. "Just a dry bit of toast with a teaspoon of butter like you like it."

I smiled and took the bread. "Please, you've been here for over a month, call me Anne."

"Yes, of course. I'm sorry. I was trained to never call my employers by their first names. I will adjust. I promise." Penelope lingered near the bookshelf. "I heard Terran say you found something unwanted in the garden."

Unwanted. I mulled over the word and then said, "Yes, unfortunately." I wondered why Terran was discussing this with the housekeeper. It was none of her business. I crunched into the toast and took another sip of the tea.

Penelope readjusted her white apron and pinned back a few escaped wisps of blond hair.

"Is there anything else?" I asked, wondering why she lingered.

She smoothed her apron, touching her twenty-something hips as she did so. "Yes, the contractors have said they would like to begin work on the upper floors. It may cause a bit of noise. I don't want you to be disturbed."

"Nonsense," I said. "The house needs to be finished by next month. That will give us plenty of time to organize everything. May is the big charity event and I'd like all the construction to be completed before then. If they need to make noise, that's fine." I couldn't finish the toast and handed her the plate.

"I'll let them know right away." Penelope slipped from the room. She had a way of being so graceful, like a ballerina. You'd never hear her coming or going.

It was only a few seconds later when Terran returned to the room, his phone in hand. "The reception out here is still a problem."

"Use the landline."

"I had to, but the connection is still weak."

"What did they say?" I inched to the edge of the chair.

"Detective Richards said he would come out personally to collect the bones."

I folded my hands in my lap and chewed my lower lip, a habit I still hadn't been able to break.

Terran pulled out a chair and sat beside me. I toyed with my engagement ring. The modest ring glistened in the glow of the fire.

When I looked up, his eyes searched mine. The moment I gazed into his, I felt the spark and love that had been there since I first saw him and had become even stronger over the last few months. He wanted us to be married. He had proposed and I had accepted without hesitation, but the thought of putting together a proper wedding was too much. My parents had only died a few months ago. We still needed time and there was no hurry.

"You still look unwell," he said. "Perhaps, we should get Dr. McCallister to come out and visit you."

"No, don't be silly. It's just the cold weather and a little too much wind on my cheeks. I need April to be here soon and the sun and flowers."

He held my hands in his and pulled me to him, kissing me deeply and cradling the back of my neck with his hand. Safe in his arms, I felt myself relax. My mind was transported to the long dark days of winter when there was little work to do outside, and we lingered for weeks in my bedroom beneath the sheets, wrapped in each other's embrace while snow dusted the window panes, and the silence made it feel as if we were in a world of our own.

A part of me wanted to slip away with him now, forget about the past and what I'd seen in the garden, but there was work to be done, and the image still lingered at the forefront of my mind.

A knock at the door pulled us apart. I turned to see Penelope escorting the contractor into the room. He held a rolled-up chart in his hand. "Sorry to interrupt," he said.

Terran stood first as Penelope left, closing the door behind her.

"I hope you've come with good news," Terran said.

"Yes," the contractor said. The short, dark-haired man tipped his hard-hat to me. "The schedule is back on track. Restoration to the attic is complete, the interior parts that were damaged from weather exposure have been repaired and all the items have been safely put back into place, the new roof is done, repairs to the foundation finalized, and now we're ready to move on to the master bedrooms."

"Can you start with Father's room first?" I couldn't wait for his old bedroom to be changed from the serious black colors he chose to something lighter and more friendly.

"That won't be a problem, except the dust may settle in the evenings and it may be unpleasant to breathe in those particles."

My hand brushed against my belly. It wouldn't be good to breathe in the dust.

"What about the library and dining room?" Terran suggested. "Those rooms are more likely to be visited by our guests during the charity event."

The contractor nodded. "Of course. I'll start there with my team and then maybe by late spring when the weather is nicer, we'll move upstairs to your bedroom."

"Then, we'll sleep on the porch or even outside," I said to Terran. "Wouldn't that be nice to camp outside by Willow Creek?"

"If you're willing to do that," Terran started, "then why shouldn't we plan to take the boat out for a few weeks? We could take a trip and avoid the whole project."

"I love it," I said, "but it must be after the charity event in May."

Terran turned to the contractor. "How does that work for you and your team?"

"Whatever works for you."

With the amount of money we were paying him and his team, I knew he wouldn't object. I clasped my hands under my chin excited at the prospect of sailing away with Terran.

The contractor then said, "There may be one problem."

My shoulders tightened at the word, problem. "Nothing that will interfere with the charity event I hope."

He waved us to follow him to the table and unrolled the master house plans on the smooth service.

I gazed at the property plans, recognizing the east and west wings clearly, the orangery, surrounding gardens, vestibules, dining rooms, kitchen, staff quarters, office, bedrooms, garage, and master bedrooms, all twenty thousand square feet of house, but then noticed a space that I couldn't recognize.

The contractor put his finger directly onto that space. "This room has been sealed off. It lies directly between the two master bedrooms in an area that may have been used as a small upstairs sitting room or perhaps a storage area."

I thought of the long hallway that separated the upstairs rooms. "I always believed it was a crawl space but you're saying it's big enough to be a room."

"Could be big enough to work for storage if you need it or you could add on another bathroom."

Terran's gaze turned toward mine and I knew what he was thinking. "A man cave," he said.

"Not in this manor home." I was already dreaming of making the space into a spa or yoga studio.

"So, you'd like the wall to be taken down?" the contractor asked.

"Yes," Terran and I said together.

Once the contractor left, Terran started right away with the benefits of having his own man cave where he could unwind after a hard day of working in the gardens.

"Oh, come on," I said. "You love working in the gardens. It's hardly work, and we've already expanded the porch for you to relax.

"It's just that ever since you gave the cottage to the new head gardener, I've lost my privacy."

His words stung. I scraped the inside of my thumb with my nail. Terran and I rarely fought. Not since it became clear that we needed each other after surviving my father's attack. I helped him heal through months of therapy. He helped me process losing my parents. We needed each other, but now it felt like he was pulling away. I didn't want Terran to ever feel like he needed to be away from me.

"Fine," I relented. "Take the room. It's not like there aren't a dozen others where you could go to get away from me."

"That's not what I meant," he said, trying to pull me back.

But it was too late. I hurried from the room. I never wanted to be a burden to anyone.

CHAPTER

TWO

I made my way through the hallways of Whitehall Manor, past vestibules, and staff dusting antique furniture to the side door that led outside and worked my way around the pathway to the driveway where I spotted my grandfather's beat-up white truck, then turned and hurried to the orangery where I knew I'd find him.

The building was a work of art. Similar to a greenhouse, it housed all of Whitehall Manor's fruit trees. The stone base and pillars made it feel as if I was stepping back in time to a Mediterranean villa. The large, tall windows faced south and maximized the sunlight in the afternoons while the north-facing walls with smaller windows kept the room warm for the tropical plants. It had been my sanctuary in the cold months. When icy-cold winds blew up the Chesapeake Bay and rattled the windows of our secluded manor home, I'd rush to the orangery to feel the trapped warmth of the sunlight on my face and Seraphine's presence all around me.

I pulled open the door and stepped inside. The air was thick with humidity. The pungent sweet scents of citrus blossoms filled my nose. A fine mist of water touched my cheeks. My mother had cultivated every corner and crevice with the most lavish of citrus and other fruits in the hopes that her father, Salazar, would visit her. Those plants had nearly died in her absence, but Salazar's loving touch brought them back to life. I hurried past a darkened grotto and three fountains to the corner of the building where he stood beneath a large thick-leaved tropical plant.

"Grandfather," I said, coming to his side and hugging him. "When did you arrive?"

"An hour ago," he said, returning the embrace.

I pushed back the few gray hairs that grew wild around his temples. His heavy work boots and pants told me he'd come from the corn fields of his own home only fifteen miles outside of the nearby town of Ashbury.

"You look stressed," he said, searching my eyes. "Come sit down."

I followed him to a stone table and chairs beside a bubbling fountain. "The orangery looks better than ever," I said. I gazed around the room taking in the red-ripe pomegranates that dangled from the nearby tree. Only feet from there an orange tree bloomed full of luscious fruit and beside that the lemon tree he rescued from near-death. It now flourished with dozens of bright yellow fruits.

"It reminds me of being back in Southern Spain," he said. "Always sunshine when you're in the orangery."

"You've outdone yourself," I said. "All this in only a few months."

"I had the saplings, but they didn't stay small for long. The trees love this room."

"The conditions are perfect."

"It's not just the Ph levels and sunlight. It's your mother. Seraphine's touch is in everything here."

I smiled knowing he was right. I could feel her beside me now.

"What troubles you?" he asked, turning my attention back to what happened only a few minutes ago.

"It seems silly," I said. "After all we've been through, I have no reason to complain."

"Small complaints can add up to bigger things. You know that."

"I do know that. I know that too well." I couldn't help but remember all the issues between my mother and father that had culminated in catastrophe. I had to deal with my problems as they came, so I took a deep breath and said, "I think I'm pregnant."

Salazar clapped his hands together and shook them to the sky. "This is not a problem. This is a blessing. Blessed be our family." His eyes welled with tears as he stood to embrace me.

"I'm not a hundred percent sure, but I feel different."

"You must let me make you something to eat. You need to eat for two."

"No, not right now. I'm a little sick."

"I'll bring you a cup of my famous broth when you're better. It has been a recipe in my family for generations. When your grandmother and I arrived from Spain to this country, she found she was pregnant with your mother, and she ate this broth with every meal. Only a short time later Seraphine was born. She was the light of our lives. The baby will be the light of your life, too."

"I promise I'll try your broth when I'm feeling better."

"Will you take good care of yourself?"

"Of course."

"You will rest, though. You work too hard. Too much

stress and you will eat the broth so you will have a baby with a full head of dark hair."

"What if I want my baby to have blond hair?"

"Nonsense." Salazar waved away the thought. "The baby will be like you with long dark hair, almond-shaped eyes, and red, rosy cheeks."

"I wanted you to be the first to know."

"Why not your husband?"

"He's not my husband," I said. "Terran and I are not married."

"You live together. You will have a baby together. You are together."

"I suppose it's going to have to work for now. I know he wants to be married. At least I think he does. I don't know. Do you think he loves me?"

He sat back stunned. "What a question."

I gnawed on my lip. "I worry we are together only because we went through something terrible. Maybe it's more convenient that we are together."

"Stop that," he said. "You stop this negative talk."

I knew why I did it. I had been sent away from White-hall Manor as a child. The feeling of loneliness and abandonment never fully left me. Now, with everything flourishing around me, I still couldn't be sure it was real.

"You will get married. You will be happy."

If only things could be that simple. "We can't be married yet, Salazar. There's too much to be done at White-hall Manor. The charity event is coming up in May. You'll be there, right?"

"Yes, of course. I'll be there to show off my famous lemon trees here in the orangery."

"The orangery is being used for the auction."

"There will be people who will come to see my lemon trees and not your auction."

I laughed at that and reached out to pluck a pomegranate for later.

"So, answer my question," he said. "Why not tell your "boyfriend" this good baby news first?"

Salazar had a way of making me want to tell the truth. I knew no matter what I said, he would love me, so I told him. "I'm not sure he wants the baby."

"Of course, he wants the baby. He's a gardener. He loves to watch things grow. He loves you. This is his life."

"I suppose you're right." I chewed on my lip and Salazar snapped at me to stop. I did and sighed. "It's just we don't know each other completely yet. We've been through a lot in the last few months, but we've never talked about having children together."

"But now you will," Salazar said. "You must confide in each other. You need each other's strength to maintain Whitehall Manor."

I knew he was right. Even with all the help, Whitehall Manor needed two strong people to sustain it. Terran led the team outside. I led the team inside. Together, we made it work. I began to think about the possibilities that I had originally wanted for Whitehall Manor. I wanted it to flourish. I wanted the community to only know it for its beauty and serenity. I needed Terran to do that. I needed him to get through the next six months and beyond.

"You will go inside and tell him after we have finished our chat," Salazar said.

I nodded. "I'll tell him," I said, and I knew I would have to but not today.

We talked all afternoon long. As the early spring sun began to set, he told me he had to get back home.

He promised to come see me in the morning with the special broth.

After giving him a long hug, I walked him to his truck and watched as he drove away from Whitehall Manor.

The March wind blew stronger, rustling the tree branches. I pulled my sweater tight and took in a deep breath of the clean air. As I turned to head back to the house, I glanced up at the space where the contractor said there was an additional room. The workers had already started pulling away the siding. It was obvious now that there was a window there that balanced out the rest of the house.

I smiled as I imagined the coming days. It wouldn't be a man-cave or a yoga room. I felt a fluttering inside of me and knew it would be the baby's room. A red-tailed hawk over-head screeched.

Just as I glanced up, it landed on the roof of the house near the newly exposed window.

My gaze trailed to what looked like a shadow reflecting from the room. One of the workers or the contractor, no doubt, or perhaps a trick on my overly anxious mind. I hurried back to the house looking forward to a cozy evening by the fire and another cup of Penelope's mint tea.

CHAPTER

THREE

D etective Richards appeared on the doorstep the next day, his head cleanly shaven and a familiar gleam in his green eyes as he waited for me to show him to the spot where I had found the bones.

I wanted to wait for Terran to return from town but knew he could be gone for hours, so I quickly grabbed my sweater and slipped on my work boots, then guided him out into the Marigold Garden.

When we reached the spot, I looked down and felt the same sinking feeling I had the day before. In the noonday sun, the grayish tint to the bones was more obvious. The skull looked more alien now than before.

"They're human bones, right?" I asked.

"Yes," the detective said. "I'd say a newborn's."

He leaned closer. "They're almost all intact. No signs of decomposition."

"What does that mean?"

Picking up one of the smallest parts, a finger bone, he examined it. "Could mean they're from an infant who died more recently."

"That's impossible. No one at Whitehall Manor has had a child."

He dropped the bone and pinched the dirt surrounding it. "Was this always a garden?" he asked.

"No. It was a field before." I tried to remember if Seraphine had written anything about the area where she planned the Marigold Garden. "I don't know exactly but Terran said he thought they planted vegetables here."

"Why does he think that?"

"We found a few things while tending to the new marigolds, a few tomato saplings and radish leaves sprung up between the bushes."

The detective nodded. "Neutral soil. It's good for growing vegetables and preserving bones."

"So, the bones could be old."

"Could be."

"When will you know?"

"As soon as the examiner tells me."

I scratched my arm. "Yes, but how long will that take?"

"Could be a few days or a few weeks."

"A few weeks?" I shook my head. "That won't work." I didn't need bad news right before the charity event. "Can you get the examiner to do it today?"

"I can try."

"Will he be able to tell me who they belonged to?"

"You want to know?"

"Of course, I want to know."

"There are tests, expensive tests, that could be run. I'd have to send them to the lab over in Chesterton. If they're genetically related to you, we could tell. Perhaps they are from long ago."

"They must be. As I said, no one has had a child here

and no one has buried a deceased infant in the garden. That would be insane."

The detective collected the pieces. With each bone he removed from the ground, the form of the infant lost its shape. Now they were just pieces of something even more lost than before.

My fingers tingled. I held my breath as the detective placed the bones into the smallest body bag I'd ever seen.

"I'm surprised they didn't get dug up by an animal," he said.

"They were buried pretty deep."

He lifted the tiny foot fragments.

I cringed and said, "I thought you scoured every inch of the property when looking for Maura Wells' body. How could you miss this?"

"We were looking for something bigger," he said. "I can't believe anyone discovered them at all. If you weren't digging out here, they may have laid there for eternity, which may be what was intended."

"You mean this spot may have been a grave?"

"Maybe not officially."

"That's impossible. Before this was a garden, it was a field. No one would have been buried without a tombstone and especially not in a field full of vegetables. The Towry family plot is on the other side of the property. Only Seraphine's ashes were laid to rest in the Marigold Garden."

I turned to see him lifting the skull from the ground. Unearthed, it looked even bigger than what I had seen before. Its empty eye sockets told the story of a child who must have suffered.

He lowered the skull into the bag.

"Maybe they're not Towry bones," I said. "Maybe they're from earlier settlers or a field hand."

"Could be." He zipped the bag. "We'll know more once we run the tests."

"I'm grateful they were found before the charity event next month. I could only imagine the guests' reactions to finding more bones on the property at Whitehall Manor. If the events that happened here weren't bad enough already. We're just starting to win back the community's trust."

With the remains secured, we began to make our way from the garden.

"And I appreciate your discretion with this," I said.

"You don't need to worry. It will be between us and the medical examiner. I'll be back once I know more." He tipped his hat and got into his car.

Once Detective Richards was gone, I walked back to the house. I pulled my sweater tighter, feeling the coldness of winter still lingering in my bones. Physical changes were happening to me whether I was ready for them or not.

Besides the morning sickness, I'd had the strangest dreams over the past few nights.

They were always similar. In my dreams, there was a man watching me from the corner of my bedroom. He sat in the darkness, in a chair with one foot crossed over his leg smoking a pipe. Always in the morning, there was a scent of strong tobacco, something sharp and acrid, lingering in the room that Terran said must be from one of the staff members who took his smoke break near our bedroom window.

There was a strange anxiety to these dreams that made it difficult to sleep. I got the feeling that the man in my nightmares didn't want me there. As if this was his dream and I was imposing on it. He frustrated me night after night with his presence until finally it dawned on me that the spiced tea I'd been drinking before bed must be the source of my fitful rest. That combined with the anxiety of processing what happened last fall must have caused me to conjure his image in my dreams.

But still days later, despite cutting out spiced tea, the man returned to my dreams. Only this time he didn't sit in the corner. He stood and made his way toward the bed where I lay unable to move, in a sort of deep sleep paralysis.

Now, I could see his face. His red, swollen cheeks and cold, black eyes glared at me, and he whispered in my ear, "Get out."

The thought of it now made shivers run down my spine. I hated to be alone, and I detested the feeling of losing control, but I feared another haunting at Whitehall Manor more than anything else. I hurried faster back to the house where I knew the warmth of the fire waited for me and Penelope's mint tea to settle my stomach.

Nearly back to the drive now, the last memory of the previous night's terror came to me. Terran gently woke me near predawn and said I had been crying in my sleep. How I wanted to tell him about the nightmare and all my fears about the pregnancy, but I didn't know for sure if it was the right time.

Did Terran want to marry me? Did he want a child with me? I couldn't risk losing him or upsetting everything we'd built together so far. Besides the charity event would be here soon and my pregnancy barely showed, so I kept my mouth shut as he massaged my back and told me that everything would be okay.

But his comfort was short-lived.

As the early morning light filtered through the blinds, I could clearly see to the corner of the room, to the armchair where the man in my nightmare had been sitting. Beside the chair, on a small wooden table something smoldered. I eased from the bed and went to it.

"What are you doing?" Terran had asked.

I couldn't believe what I was seeing. Ash from smoked tobacco. It had scarred the wood of the table. I tipped the water from the flower vase onto it, dousing the smoke. Then, I felt a shudder pass through me.

"Come back to bed," Terran said. "It's too early."

I did as he said, hurrying to get beneath the bedsheets where I thought I'd be safe.

FOUR

That afternoon I sat in Doctor McCormick's office waiting for the pregnancy results. The more I thought about it, the more obvious it was that I would soon be a mother. Already my breasts were tender and there was no denying that I'd felt light-headed and queasy in the mornings.

Dr. McCormick gently knocked on the door and came into the room.

I attempted to cover myself with the flimsy hospital gown to the best of my ability. The horrible smell of anti-septic lingered in the air.

The doctor was tall and thin. He had light brown hair, gray eyes, and deep wrinkles around his eyes. Before I could say hello, he said, "You're about three months pregnant."

My eyes widened. I felt a flutter in my chest.

He wrote something on my chart as I tried to compose myself.

"I should have come sooner."

"It would have been ideal, but we can get started on your nutrition and testing now."

He helped me to lean back and pressed his cold hands on my abdomen.

"I honestly wasn't sure if I was pregnant," I said. "I mean until recently I couldn't even tell."

"Your first pregnancy can be a bit tricky but there's definitely something growing here."

Guiding my hands to the spot, he showed me where to feel. I pressed on my womb where he held his hands and felt a small mound.

My hands began to shake. "I wasn't prepared for this. I mean I never thought I'd have children. Not this way."

"What way is that?" the doctor asked.

I felt my cheeks redden. "It's so fast. I thought maybe someday I'd have children but ..." My thoughts trailed off as I realized how Terran and I had found our way to lovemaking nearly every day after things settled down. We clung to each other in all the change.

"What now?" I asked.

"You'll need to come back for checkups, make sure to eat healthy, and avoid stress."

I laughed. "That's impossible. My house is being renovated. My parents both died only a few months ago. I'm not even married. I'm having a charity event in May, and—"

He raised a brow.

I wanted to say that baby bones had been unearthed in one of my gardens but bit my lip instead. "I guess I need to relax, huh?"

He nodded and wrote something else in my chart. "You'll be fine. All new mothers feel nervous. Do you have help?"

"Oh, yes." If there was anything I did have, it was help. I had a whole staff of help at Whitehall Manor, six staff inside, and six gardeners outside, then, of course, there was Terran and my grandfather, Salazar.

As the doctor began the full exam, my mind drifted to worries about the baby's health. I couldn't shake the image of the alien-like head in the garden. Could a few glasses of wine over the last few weeks cause that to happen? My mind jumped next to all the vitamins I was supposed to be taking during the first trimester.

Dr. McCormick angled the video monitor toward me and began clicking something.

"Are you running tests?" I asked. "To make sure everything is okay?"

"No, just taking pictures."

"Pictures?" I struggled to shift to my elbows.

"Relax," he said.

I lowered back down. "Will you run blood tests?"

"We'll do all the standard ones."

"And check for deformities?"

"Are you talking about genetic testing?"

I nodded. "There's a history of illness in my family." I thought of the bones again and shivered. "I want to make sure everything is normal."

"From what I'm seeing, everything looks fine. Look here."

Turning my head, I gazed at the computer monitor. My eyes widened. I was staring at the shadowy outline of a baby the size of a plum, my baby. Its heartbeat and fluids pulsed inside its sac. I took a deep breath and felt something deep inside of me shift. Completeness overwhelmed me. I was no longer alone in the world. Tears slipped down my cheeks to the table.

Dr. McCormick smiled as he put away the ultrasound

device. "We can always run other tests, more invasive ones if you're concerned."

"No." I sat up feeling suddenly protective of my body and child. "I just wanted to make sure."

"If you change your mind, let me know."

After the full exam ended, I hurried to change and made my way out to my car. I nervously laughed as I thought of the future. All the death and despair felt mollified with the good news. A baby was on the way. The spring was nearly here and so was the life growing inside of me. I pressed the back of my hand to my cheek and gazed at my reflection in the mirror. There was real joy in my eyes for the first time in months. I had nothing to fear and nothing to worry about but no matter how much I tried to focus on everything that was good, I had the lingering feeling that the rug would be pulled out from under me at any moment.

I shook it away and hurried back to Whitehall Manor. It was time to tell Terran the news. I shouldn't wait until after the charity event. Our relationship was surely strong enough, but would he want to get married immediately? Would he want to postpone the charity event to organize a wedding reception?

It was wrong to withhold the information. The charity event was important. It was the moment Whitehall Manor would finally shine again, but to think I could keep a secret like my pregnancy for five months was ridiculous. As I drove onto the road that would take me to Whitehall, I made up my mind to tell Terran. No matter what happened I would be okay. I had a child to be with me forever, a blessing like Salazar said.

CHAPTER
FIVE

The next day, Penelope woke me with breakfast in bed. Two eggs on dry toast with a teaspoon of butter and instead of spiced tea, a little warm milk with a hint of something nutritious blended into it that I requested the previous day.

She went to the windows and pulled back the curtains as I stretched my arms overhead. The space where Terran slept was empty. I hadn't seen him when I returned, and he never made it to bed.

Outside the wind blew, still typical of March along the eastern seaboard, and a slight chill lingered in the air making me wonder if the fire in the sitting room had gone out. Only a few more weeks until I could fling open the windows and enjoy the fresh air of Willow Creek and not worry about layering sweaters or wearing my heavy coat to keep warm when I ventured outside.

Penelope fluffed the blanket that she laid softly across my legs as I ate my breakfast.

"Did Terran say where he was going this morning?" I asked her.

"I believe he said he would be working to prepare the garden. Something about getting rid of last year's old growth and preparing the soil for the new season."

She moved to the side table and collected a vase of wilted flowers.

I didn't want to raise suspicions in the household, but I couldn't take my eyes off the side of the bed where he slept. "Did you see him last night?" I asked.

Penelope stopped what she was doing and turned to me. "Last night?"

"Yes, I didn't see him at dinner. Did he sleep on the porch again? I know how he loves it out there."

"I'm not sure," she said. "Perhaps. Would you like me to check with him?"

"No," I said. "I'll ask him. I was just wondering."

There was a sudden tension in the room between us that I couldn't understand. I had asked her a simple question. I decided to shift the conversation. "And the contractor?" I asked. "Will he be by today?"

"Yes, he called and said he will be here by noon to finish the work on the spare room," she said, taking the empty vase from the bureau and disappearing into the bathroom.

I couldn't wait to see what the room looked like. So far, the door had been cut, but no one was allowed inside until they finished framing it and cleaning up their mess. I gazed out the window to Willow Creek. A heron sat perched on a pilon. The soft birdsong relaxed me as I thought of my child growing inside me.

Penelope returned to the room with a vase of yellow tulips she said had come up early in the garden and placed them next to my bed. They weren't the same as fresh marigolds but would have to do.

"The flowers are lovely," I said.

Her grin showed perfectly small white teeth like two rows of baby pearls. Her soft pink lipstick shimmered in the morning light and matched the respectable soft glimmer of the taupe eyeshadow that dusted her eyelids. Even her scent was fresh like peonies and jasmine.

She worked her way around the room picking up clothes I had tossed to the ground the previous evening.

"Is there anything else you need?" she asked, retrieving the rest of the laundry from the basket.

"How are things going with the charity event?"

"The invitations went out last week and so far, over one hundred people have responded that they're coming."

"One hundred? I didn't realize it would be so well-received."

"Oh, yes. Everyone is talking about the party at White-hall Manor. I wouldn't be surprised if you had over three hundred people coming."

"Three hundred?" I sat up letting my fork clank to the plate.

"Don't worry," Penelope said. "I will take care of everything. There will be food and drinks for everyone. The staff know their duties and we'll bring in extra people to park the cars and ferry the passages who come by boat. There's a string quartet booked and Terran said the gardens would be open and ready for viewing. He's even prepared a little lecture on the various types of marigolds he's growing this year. It will be a lovely party."

He hadn't told me that. I rubbed the back of my neck wondering why he hadn't shared his lecture notes with me. I reminded myself to ask him about them. Perhaps the guests would want to hear about Seraphine and her tireless effort to grow the garden.

"You look much better today," she said.

I relaxed. "Yes, ever since I gave up the spiced tea at night, I've been sleeping better. That seems to help." I blew out a breath. "Plus, you've been a lifesaver getting everything together for the party. You are a miracle worker."

"Well, there's one thing I can't do."

I knew immediately to what she was referring. "The auction."

She nodded. "We need items from the attic."

"Yes," I took another sip of the warm milk. I had been putting that off for as long as I could. I would have to go up into the attic and through the family heirlooms to find a few things worth auctioning, but the thought of stepping foot up there since seeing Father descend into total madness sent a ripple of fear through me.

"If you'd like, I can go up there with you."

"No." I put down the cup and pushed off the blankets. "I have to face my fears on my own. I've been through much worse than simply going into an attic."

"Are you sure?"

"Yes," I said, swinging my legs over the side of the bed. "You continue to respond to our guests and make the preparations. I'll find something in the attic, a few heirlooms of Whitehall Manor's past that people might want to pay for."

As soon as I was dressed and Penelope had left, I focused on the door at the end of the hallway that led to the attic. It was just a room. A room with old stuff stored in it.

I flicked on the light that illuminated the staircase. If only this had been working months ago so I didn't have to venture up the creaking stairs into the pitch dark, but that was all behind me. Now, the attic was remodeled with working heat and electricity. I slowly walked up the stairs. Despite months of remodeling to the house, including the attic and roof, the stairs still creaked with each step. I turned the corner at the top and gasped. It was the first time I'd seen the attic since the repairs. It was nothing like what I remembered.

Above me, the ceiling was fully plastered. I remembered when I could see all the way up to the stars and stood on old boxes to get a breath of fresh air. I turned my gaze to the alcoves where I had found Father. As I walked to that portion of the attic, I stopped and took a breath. The lingering scent of mold and wet wood was gone. The old trunks, paintings, and heirlooms still filled the open spaces but were organized and covered in white tarps from the painters.

I pulled off one tarp to see a stack of oil paintings. Each one depicted a scene of the Towry family from hundreds of years ago. There were images of men in pantaloons and triangle hats with ruffled vests and long coats. Women in long flourishing dresses with small dogs at their heels and children dressed like small adults.

The same Towry stare gleamed in each of their faces along with strong jawlines and focused gazes. These could sell for a fortune, but they were too important to auction off. I draped them with tarps again. At least the air temperature was controlled now so whatever had survived the roof cave-in was now not at risk of further deterioration.

So much though hadn't survived the years of rain and mold. The workers ended up throwing out heirlooms that were beyond repair including many old books, stenciled drawings, and moth-eaten tapestries.

Walking further down the long space, I came to the alcove where I found Father. I shuddered at the memory of Lucinda Warner's dead body beside him, the crazed glare in his eyes, and the horrible stench lingering from dead animals he captured and killed for food. The Towry curse reverberated in my head along with the reminder that Samuel Towry had been facing a steady decline for years until he sank into total madness.

I pushed past the alcove to parts of the attic that I had not visited before and that had been impossible to get to after the west wing chimney caved in. Around the corner, I suddenly realized that I was moving toward the part of the house where the original vents were still in place. There was the spot where my mother, Seraphine, had been crying for help and warning me to leave before it was too late. All of that was over now. There was no going back. No saving my mother from her death or fixing what was forever broken.

At the end of the alcove was an old sewing machine, mirror, sculptures, figurines, and a wardrobe. Beside the closet was a bucket full of scrolls and an old sword with a faded gold tassel. I took one of the scrolls and opened it recognizing I was looking at the original house plans for Whitehall Manor. These would be desirable to a local architect or even the archives in Ashbury. I laid them aside and shifted my gaze to the wardrobe.

Slowly opening the doors, a delicious scent of cedar wood lifted into the air. I took a deep inhale of the warm, smooth scent that reminded me of Terran's aftershave. Then, I shifted my gaze to the centuries old clothing that had not been destroyed by rodents or moths.

I felt the cloth of the silk dresses knowing they must have come from the seventeen hundreds. At the bottom of the cabinet's floor were shoes made for women with feet much smaller than mine and on the top were a few dusty boxes that contained women's wigs. I couldn't help but stare at the dark-haired wig with a side braided ponytail and laugh wondering what I would look like in all this finery.

There was only one way to find out. I quickly slipped out of my jeans and t-shirt and chose one of the silk dresses from the closet, a crimson gown with a ruffled hem and plunging neckline. The cinched waist would never work for my expanding belly but everything else fit perfectly. Next, I grabbed the wig and slipped it onto my head, tucking my hair into it. I gazed into the wardrobe mirror.

Now, I looked like the lady of the manor. I walked from the mirror and back imagining how it must have been for the women back in the day. Sitting in this dress in the hot muggy summer must have been torture and wearing a dress as fitted as this while pregnant was out of the question but there was also something comforting about it. I twirled and admired the stitching. It was another work of art. Whitehall Manor held many secrets, but it held just as many rewards.

All of this would be wonderful to auction off. I could only imagine a real collector's eyes lighting up the moment they saw the fine stitching and beadwork of the dresses. I bundled several dresses into a pile on an old wooden chair and searched the wardrobe for something else worth auctioning off.

At the bottom of the cabinet was a shelf. I lowered down and felt something at the back and pulled out a wooden box not bigger than a shoebox. I blew an inch of dust off the top and sneezed.

There was no lock, only a latch to secure it closed. I pried open the top and gazed inside at the softest red silk lining and a folded piece of paper.

Curiosity got the best of me as I reached to unfold it. The paper was so old and brittle that it practically disintegrated in my hands, but I was able to save it by going slowly and laying it as flat as I could on the attic floor.

The cursive writing had an interesting style. Each letter had an old-fashioned curve to the penmanship. I examined the document to see it was a legal document, a will, written in the eighteen hundreds showing the inheritor of Whitehall Manor to be a Thomas Towry.

Last Will and Testament
October 21, 1881

I, Caroline Towry, am of sound mind and body, despite what has been proclaimed in court by my brother John Burton Towry who has been found guilty of his crimes and is in fact of a most demented mind hence his institution at the Baltimore Asylum for the Criminally Insane.

I do declare that the entire of my estate should be left to my only surviving son, Thomas Towry, who at this time is only one month of age and in the care of my great aunt Dorothea Barrow, however, upon his eighteenth birthday, he should lay claim to Whitehall Manor in its entirety. It is not without much resentment that I must make this will, due to my deteriorating health which will undoubtedly be my undoing by year's end if not sooner.

-Caroline Towry

The hair lifted at the nape of my neck as I slowly folded the paper and put it back into the box. My mind flashed to when I'd first heard of something called the Towry Curse. It was during my research into Maura Wells' disappearance. A whole online forum had been set up to discuss the cursed Towrys. I recalled the words mentioning mental illness and an unusual form of schizophrenia wrote one doctor. I closed the box and shoved it back into the shelf knocking something down from a higher ledge that landed beside me.

My breath stopped. Beside me was a leather-bound journal with worn edges that reminded me of the same type of diary my mother kept. Just looking at it made my muscles tense. I slid away from it. There was no way I would open it. I needed Whitehall Manor's past to stay in the past. I wanted to shove it back into the wardrobe, bury it deep enough so that no one would ever find it, but something stopped me. What if there was something in the journal about the bones in the garden? What if there were clues to the supposed Towry curse?

I was being silly and sat back and laughed. It was probably just a ledger of some kind or a record of daily high and low tides. I picked up the book and shifted closer to the window where the sun had finally broken through some clouds and shone through to the attic floor. Sitting in that beam of light, I opened the journal. The penmanship was starkly different from what I had read in Caroline Towry's will.

The lettering was frantic. As my eyes scanned the words a tremor started in me that I couldn't stop. There was something evil in the words I read, something that awakened something in me that I didn't recognize. It was as if in those seconds of glancing at the journal entry, I had slipped deep into a forgotten well of time, possessed by something stronger than myself.

CHAPTER
SIX

"Anne?"

I was startled at the sound of Penelope's voice, turning quickly to see her standing only two feet behind me.

"You scared me," I said, pressing a hand to my chest.

"I'm sorry," she said. "You were so focused. I didn't want to disturb you." Her eyes flashed to the dress I wore. "I love this." She stepped to me and touched the fabric. "Silk?"

I quickly stood. "Yes, I forgot I still had it on."

"Oh, it's beautiful and fits you nicely," she said, examining my waistline.

I couldn't help but notice her eyes widen as if she suddenly knew my baby secret. She quickly changed the topic. "Were you reading something important?" Her gaze shifted to the journal in my hand. "I came up to see if you were okay. You've been up here for several hours."

"Hours?"

"Yes, the contractor is nearly finished with his work. He was wondering if you wanted to take a look at the room. The framing is done."

"Yes," I said, staring at the journal.

"Are you okay?"

"I-I'm fine," I said as I returned the journal to the wardrobe.

She examined me for a moment and then turned her attention to the dresses on the chair. "Oh, these are lovely. They will sell at the charity event. I can think of at least ten people, including Mrs. Callahan who will fight to the death to get one of these. And the wigs."

"Be careful," I said. "They're fragile. They've been up here for a while."

"Yes, we should have them sealed in something to preserve them." She searched through the cabinet and pulled out a few other items. "These books look like first editions."

"Yes, you should take them. I'm sure they'll do well at auction."

"I'm amazed the rats and insects didn't turn all of this into a nest." Penelope carefully took several of the dresses and laid them on her arm. "I'll come back for the rest," she said. "These are great choices."

Before she turned to leave, I stopped her. "I'll bring down the rest, okay?"

"Of course."

"It's just that so much of what's up here are family heirlooms and—"

"You don't have to say anything more." Penelope smiled. "I take my orders from you, Anne. If you don't want me up here, I won't come up here." She turned and headed down the path toward the stairs.

I picked up a few wigs. I stared at the journal again. It needed to stay in the attic, far away from anyone's eyes. I surveyed the remaining collection of items and managed to carry two sculptures that I was sure would need to be appraised before auction, if not sent to a museum.

After several more trips up and down the attic stairs, carrying more heirlooms and other artifacts of Towry history, I decided there were plenty of items in front of us that would sell well or at least satisfy the locals' strong curiosity about Whitehall Manor for a while. I slipped out of the red gown and back into my too-tight jeans and t-shirt, then headed toward the spare room to take a look at the contractor's work.

I could hardly believe my eyes. The room smelled of old wood that had been sealed up for over a hundred years. A nearly faded yellow wallpaper covered the walls. I bent to touch the flooring, unscratched and preserved it hadn't buckled or warped in all this time despite the lack of maintenance. I stepped to the window and gazed down to the driveway wondering if this room was Whitehall Manor's way of welcoming my child.

It would be an ideal space for a baby, not too far from the master bedroom, and with a few coats of paint and baby-proofing, it would be perfect.

"How do you like the room?" the contractor asked as he stepped into the room.

"It's wonderful. Why would anyone board this up?"

"That's a good question," he said. "Maybe the owner didn't need the expense of heating another room."

"They could've closed the door. Why go to all the fuss of concealing the window as well?"

The contractor shrugged. "All I know is that it was a child's room."

"How do you know?"

He led me to the closet. Inside, he pointed to drawings on the back wall.

I stepped closer and examined the crude figures drawn with a charcoal pencil. The image showed a girl hanging by her neck from a tree. "What is this?"

"A child's sick imagination," he said. "We also found a jack in the box," he said. "In the corner of the closet. Want to see it?"

I nodded and he led me across the hall to where the other workers were cleaning up for the day. On the table was the box. I picked it up admiring the painted picture along its side of a girl and boy skipping toward what looked like a witch's house. I shuddered. "It's creepy."

"Must be from the eighteen hundreds." He took the box and turned the crank. The nerve-wracking tune of "Pop Goes the Weasel" played as I folded my hands in front of me and braced myself. After several cranks, nothing happened.

"Huh," the contractor said. "Worked for us earlier."

"Well, it's old. I'm surprised it worked at all."

The contractor put the box on the table when suddenly the lid lifted and a foot-long clown burst forward.

I screamed and clutched a hand to my chest as the contractor laughed.

"That's terrifying," I said.

"They don't make toys this good anymore."

"Well, you can have it if you want it."

"Really? Sure. Thanks."

"You've done an excellent job with the spare room. Thank you for working so quickly. I'll need the wallpaper stripped of course and the walls painted a nice neutral color, but the flooring is perfect."

"I'll get my workers on it tomorrow."

Once I had finished with the contractor, I headed toward the sitting room and scanned our haul of heirlooms from the attic.

A moment later Terran came through the doorway, a smudge of dirt on his cheek.

"Where have you been?" I asked.

"In the garden," he said, taking a drink from his bottled water. "You know I work in the garden in the morning."

I wanted to ask him about last night but before I could say anything he said, "Detective Richards is here."

"Already? I thought it would take days if not weeks until I heard from him." I hurried to the front door where the detective stood in the hallway.

"Good afternoon," he said, removing his hat revealing his cleanly shaven head.

"Detective Richards, you're here sooner than I thought." I pulled back my shoulders. "With no warrant for anyone's arrest, I hope."

The familiar scent of alpine lingered around him. "No. You were right. The bones aren't from a recent death."

I blew out a breath. "Come to the sitting room," I said, helping him with his coat and hat.

Once back in the room, I followed his gaze to see him looking at the items for the auction. "You will be coming to the charity event, won't you?"

"My wife and I have already sent our RSVP. Looking forward to seeing something good happen out here."

"You were a great help in getting me through the worst time of my life." I couldn't help but remember how he showed up for me at the hospital and reassured me through the darkest hours after Father's death. "Would you like some tea?"

"Coffee would be great," he said. "No sugar. I'm trying to watch my weight."

I nodded to Penelope who quickly made her way through the door to the kitchen.

Terran shook the detective's hand. "Thanks for coming out so quickly."

I sat in the chair by the fire. "I can hardly wait to hear what you have to tell us. I haven't been able to stop thinking about the bones. Do you have answers for us?"

"The only thing I can tell you is that the bones are not from this generation."

My eyes went to Terran's and we both relaxed. "Thank goodness for that. I don't think I could handle another investigation at Whitehall."

"No, there won't be anything like what happened before. It would be hard to investigate a possible crime from a hundred-fifty years ago."

"A hundred fifty years?" Terran said.

"If not more."

Terran inched forward in his chair.

"And no one knows about the bones?" I asked.

"Just as I told you, only myself and the pathologist."

I blew out a breath.

Penelope entered the room with the coffee on a tray and a few treats. She placed them on the table between us and then quietly exited.

"What do you think?" I asked the detective as I poured him a cup of coffee. "Could they be from a Towry?"

"The only thing I can say for sure at this point is that since the bones are deformed, the baby would not have lived more than a few days." He took the mug and sipped. "Oh, this is good coffee."

I recalled seeing the deformed bones. The way the spinal cord twisted and the large, alien-like look of the eye sockets.

"Whoever the child belonged to must have known," Terran said. "I've heard that babies who are born and not expected to live were sometimes left out in the cold to die."

"That's cruel," I said, reaching for a pillow to hold in my lap.

The detective lowered his mug. "Terran's right. That was a practice many people used to hasten the death of the child."

"Maybe someone left the baby out in the cold to die," I said, "but why wouldn't they have buried the baby in the cemetery along with the other Towry family members? It must have belonged to a field hand or servant."

"This is not the first time I've been called to investigate baby bones in a field," the detective said. "Unfortunately, it may have been a servant's child or if there wasn't time to have the child baptized, they may have felt the child's soul was doomed to hell and left it apart from the others."

"Oh, that's horrible," I said, wringing my hands. "First the child is born with such horrible deformities and then cast to an unmarked grave alone." All I could think of was that poor child's soul wandering the manor for eternity.

"Don't let it upset you," the detective said, taking a cookie from the tray and biting into what looked like the chef's famous lemon meringues.

"What will happen to the bones?" Terran asked.

"I'll return them to you to be buried if that's your wish. There's a forensic anthropologist in Washington D.C. I could bring over to reconstruct the exact cause of death."

"No," I said. "That's not necessary." I fidgeted thinking about the extra attention that might bring. "I think the child was born with deformities and if it is as you say over a hundred fifty years ago, they wouldn't have had the means to care for a sick baby. Still, the child deserves a proper burial."

"I agree," Terran said.

"That's settled then," I said. "We'll have the baby buried in the Towry cemetery. I don't care if it's a Towry child or not. The child deserves to be buried properly."

Detective Richards put down his cup. His eyes flicked to the pillow I clutched.

I swallowed and laid it aside as he shifted his gaze to the dresses on the table. "Are these what you're putting up for auction?"

"Oh, we'll have other things to bid on besides dresses," I said.

The detective's eye fell on the old sword. "Civil War," he said. "A cavalry sword."

"Is that what it is?"

"Made of pure steel. You must have had ancestors who fought in the war. Any other weapons up there in the attic?"

"Not that I saw," I said, "but if you're interested in wigs, we have plenty of those."

Terran muffled a laugh as the detective shook a finger at me and began to walk from the room. "I'm glad you've found your sense of humor."

I smiled and led him toward the door, handing him his hat and coat before opening the door to the gray outside.

While I waited for him to return with the child's bones, I stared at the end of the property where two foxes played in the light fog near the oldest tree on the property. Beyond that was the iron gate that surrounded the property. In the dusky afternoon, it was hard to see anything more except the road that narrowed to a pinpoint, but just as the detective turned from his car and began to walk toward me, I was sure I spotted someone outside the gate. A woman in a long white gown with hair that blew in the wind. She stood too far away to know anything more.

"Here you go," he said, handing me the bag.

My gaze shifted for a second and when I looked back the woman was gone.

"You know that coffee was damn good. Do you know what brand it is?"

"What?" I asked.

"The coffee. Is it one of those foreign brands?"

"I-I don't know."

"Are you alright, Ms. Towry?" the detective asked.

"Yes, why do people keep asking me that?"

"You looked lost for a second."

"Lost?" I refocused on the bag in my hands. "Oh, no. I thought I saw something. I'll make sure the bones are laid to rest properly."

The detective tipped his hat. "I get the feeling Whitehall Manor has finally got the right owner."

I smiled wondering if that was true.

Once he was gone, I called to Penelope to bring me one of the hat boxes. She met me outside and together we placed the small bones into the soft pink cushion of the box and closed it.

"Would you like me to get Terran to go with you?" she asked.

I shook my head. I'd learned to do so much on my own. I could manage this. As I gazed up at the sky, I saw it was on the brink of rain. I'd have to hurry.

The Towry family cemetery was beyond the sculpture garden in the far east corner of the property. As I carried the box in one hand and a shovel from the gardener's toolshed in the other, I thought about how my parents never allowed me to visit the cemetery as a child. They always said it was too far, too morose, or inappropriate for a child, meanwhile, Father was doing the most inappropriate things possible with other women while Mother sat idly by, hoping to win him back.

Being alone at Whitehall Manor was so rare now with all the staff who worked all day to prepare meals, clean rooms, and attend to daily washing, polishing, and cleaning. The outdoor staff, a team of six, worked in the winter, cutting back branches, maintaining the shoreline from erosion, and making the much-needed plans to prepare the gardens for the spring under Terran's direction.

Already a few daffodils and other buds poked through the ground. It wouldn't be long until all of Whitehall Manor came alive again, most importantly the Marigold Garden. I attempted to wave to one of the gardeners hard at work edging a pathway to the sculpture garden and continued on.

A short ten-minute walk later, the gate surrounding the cemetery loomed ahead. I swung open the gate and stepped through. It screeched and the crooked lower edge stuck into the grass. It was a fraction of the size of the iron gate and fencing that surrounded the entire property of Whitehall extending like two arms around the land all the way to the shoreline of Willow Creek.

It was impossible to ignore the most recent grave. My gaze fell directly on Father's resting place. The grass hadn't had a chance to grow yet. It was a simple tombstone with his name, Samuel Towry, and the years of his life. The rose I had laid there three months ago was now nothing more than a stick with thorns.

I placed the box on a nearby stone bench and lowered the shovel to the ground. It had been too long since I visited Father's grave. I wondered if he'd be happy for me now that I was going to have a baby. Was he ever proud of me?

A part of me believed he had been well when I was born. It was only when the illness set in that he changed and committed those atrocities. Killing Maura Wells, Lucinda Warner, and Seraphine was the worst of it, but it could easily have been me, too.

The guilt of his death still weighed heavily on me. How could I forget the events that led to me having to kill my own father? The memory of his gaunt and naked body running toward me, the crazed look in his eyes, and the blood from Lucinda Warner still smeared across his face. No matter how many times Terran told me it wasn't my fault, I couldn't push past wishing that I had thought of a different way to stop him.

Thunder rumbled above and light droplets of rain fell dampening my face.

Turning from his grave, I scanned the others, remembering the few times I broke the rules and visited the cemetery.

There were my favorites of course. One tombstone soared six feet high and was shaped like an obelisk. It was the grave of one of my ancestors who undoubtedly wanted to be remembered. The etched dates went as far back as the late sixteen hundreds.

My favorite tombstone was the angel-shaped marble statue, a beautifully designed white angel that had over the decades turned gray but still hovered, open-winged over its grave. Perhaps one of the reasons I adored this one was that the angel was headless. As a child, I had always believed I'd find the head hidden somewhere but never did. It remained a mystery and I accepted I'd never find it.

I stepped to it and read the headstone.

Caroline Towry
1840-1881

Here was the woman who had been Whitehall Manor's owner. My mind flashed to the will I had found in the attic. The years on the document corresponded with the ones on the headstone. She had died just as she thought she would in 1881, which was almost one hundred and fifty years ago.

I walked past the graves checking the other headstones.

Several graves crowded together in certain years where there must have been a virus or epidemic of some sort, killing four Towry members in one year of 1799, and then several more twenty years later in 1819.

I continued to walk until I found in the furthest corner

of the cemetery a crooked headstone barely noticeable beneath the foliage with the years *1838-1921* inscribed on the plaque and the name *John Burton Towry* above that. Brushing back a few branches covering the weathered headstone, I read the inscription: "May God have mercy on your soul."

My shoulders tightened. I stepped back. The words on the document referred to him as well. I recalled them exactly. *My brother, John Burton Towry, who has been found guilty of his crimes and is in fact of a most demented mind hence his institution at the Baltimore Asylum for the Criminally Insane.* This was a sick man. I knew it. It was his journal that fell from the wardrobe shelf and made me shiver to my core. A few of the words I had read tumbled through my head and I quickly shook them away. I had read enough to feel entranced to a dark part of my mind I never wanted to see again.

Glancing at the other nearby headstones, my gaze fell on one other name.

Thomas Towry
1881-1923

I swept a few wet leaves from the top of his simple and modest headstone. He had been the owner of Whitehall Manor after his mother, Caroline, and lived to only forty-two years of age. All three people mentioned in the will were buried right here, a whole generation of Towrys.

Curiosity gnawed at me. I wanted to know more about Caroline and her son, Thomas. I wanted to know why Caroline had written that she was resentful and why Thomas had died only in his forties.

I couldn't help but imagine what it must have been like

to live at Whitehall Manor at that time. There wouldn't have been electricity to the house, not even in the late years of Thomas's life, not this far out. Candlelight would have been all they had in the evenings. Well, that and the stars.

They would have been isolated from the rest of the world. Travel by road would have been limited. I knew everything would be done by boat. All trips to Baltimore and beyond would be by water. How different and strange it must have been to see a bay full of sailboats and steamers instead of highways full of cars and trucks.

The rain had picked up. My hair wetted to my face. I hurried back to the box. It, too, was getting wet, and I had to hurry to get it into the ground before the rain turned from a drizzle to a downpour.

There was only one logical choice of where I should bury the baby. It would have to be in the small space beside Caroline's grave.

I picked up the shovel. Digging several feet took time. My heart raced. I wished I had brought gloves as the wood from the shovel had started a blister on the interior of my thumb.

Once the hole was deep enough, I retrieved the box and buried it beneath the wet earth. "Now you're not alone," I said.

Suddenly, a horrible screech echoed. My eyes darted to the tree branch only six feet or so above me where a red-tailed hawk perched on a limb watching me this whole time. Its narrow, beady eyes glared down.

"You're a sly one, aren't you," I said.

I refocused my attention on smoothing the dirt on top of the box when suddenly the hawk swooped down, landing on top of me. I fell back and shielded my head feeling its sharp talons scrape my arm and head. Blood trickled down my wrist as I frantically waved my hand to get it away. "Leave me alone!" I yelled.

The bird was relentless in its attack. It screeched again and dug into me.

Beside me was a rock. I reached for it and threw it at the vicious bird. It hit its wing. The hawk screeched, its sound like nails on a chalkboard. With each passing moment its scream grew louder, a horrible ear-piercing noise that made me cover my ears. It opened its mouth to hiss at me and then lifted back to a higher branch.

"What on earth?" I slowly stood. My wet jeans were covered in mud.

In all my life, I'd never been attacked by a bird and never a hawk. I turned to look around wondering if there was a small rodent lurking nearby or a nest it was protecting. When I couldn't find anything, I couldn't help but glance back to the covered mound of dirt beside Caroline's grave and wonder if I had done something I shouldn't have.

CHAPTER
EIGHT

T hurried back to the house. It was after five o'clock now and the sky had grown darker. Above, the clouds pulled together and thickened. Rumbles of thunder grew louder overhead. About halfway back to the house, the rain poured, soaking me to my core. My teeth chattered as I sloshed through puddles thick with mud and grass. A musky freshness surrounded me. Once back at the house, I tossed the shovel to the ground and shoved open the front door.

"Penelope, I need towels." My voice echoed back to me. I felt like a drowned rat as I shook off my coat and tried to hang it on the hook beside the door. My feet stiffened in the cold as I tore off my boots and peeled off my soaking socks leaving a pool of water that mingled with blood dripping from my wounded arm.

"Is anyone here?" I called again but no one answered.

The staff had gone for the day and the stillness of the house felt unsettling. I hurried to my bedroom to remove the rest of my wet clothes, stopping short when ahead of me my gaze fell directly on the attic door swung wide open.

I stopped in the hallway taking in a short breath of air. I rubbed the back of my neck. A sharp pain pulsed on top of my head. I still held the fear that Father would descend the staircase in his maddened state and attack me. It was silly. I had left it open when collecting everything for the auction. I rushed to the door and closed it.

Making my way to the shower, I stripped off the rest of my wet clothes and turned on the warm water. Once it was hot enough, I stepped in. The water at my feet turned red. The cuts on my arm had stopped bleeding. I searched my scalp and quickly found the other source of the bleeding. The hawk's beak had broken the skin on the top of my head.

The cut wasn't big but bled terribly. I pressed the wash-cloth to the cut, hoping it would stop. As I stood there letting the warmth of the water cascade over my body, I began to feel woozy. I steadied myself against the shower wall.

The longer I stayed in the shower, the stranger I felt. I closed my eyes, swaying gently. As I rocked from foot to foot, my mind grew scattered. I gripped the towel rack feeling as if I was being watched. I opened my eyes to a black shadow passing by the shower door. I gasped and hurried to switch off the water.

"Terran?" I called out.

There was no answer. I flung open the shower door and wrapped myself in a towel.

"Penelope?"

The steam in the room had thickened making it hard to see. The same feeling as in my nightmare returned to me, the sensation of being watched. There was someone or something here.

I flicked on the exhaust fan and ran my hand over the steamed mirror. I gazed into my eyes, hardly recognizing myself. Blood cascaded down my face. I stared unable to move for several seconds as more trickles of blood dripped to my chin and dribbled to the floor. Horror filled me as I searched for a clean washcloth and pressed it again to my wound.

Where was Penelope when I needed her? I searched for my phone and found it near the bed.

"Come to the bedroom," I texted Terran.

The message didn't go through. I would have to sit here until the bleeding stopped or make my way downstairs to find them. I quickly dressed and then worked my way from the master bedroom to the hallway where my eye fell on the attic door. Again, it was open.

"Terran?" I called out. Only silence. The hallway was ice cold. I eased to the door to shut it. It chilled against my palm. As I began to shut it, a noise from above rattled me. I was brought immediately back to last autumn when the scratching and crying sounds disturbed me to my core.

I opened the door wide and flicked on the light. A breeze brushed past me. I took a breath. There had to be a window open. I slowly climbed the stairs.

At the landing, I scanned the long hallway and made my way to each alcove inspecting the windows. Finally, toward the end of the room, I spotted the half-opened window, letting in the rain that pooled along the windowsill and dripped onto the floor. I slammed it closed.

When I turned, another icy breeze pushed past me. I cringed and held my breath. The sensation made my toes curl. I suddenly didn't want to be alone. Not in the attic. Not at Whitehall. I wrapped my hands around my waist letting the washcloth fall to the floor and eased toward the stairs. Something stopped me from moving forward.

It felt separate from me and yet I knew whatever it was

that lingered only inches away was trying to enter my thoughts. It was pushing against my head and digging into my memories.

"Get away!" I screamed.

The voice whispered for me to leave.

"I won't leave," I said. "This is my home."

"*My home*," it whispered back.

I clenched my fingers. "Who are you?" I demanded.

There was only silence.

Whatever lurked in the attic was a coward. The moment the thought passed through my head, the doors to the wardrobe slammed open nearly breaking at the hinges.

My chin trembled. I took a breath and walked toward the journal on the shelf. "Is this what you want me to read?"

Silence.

I lowered the journal to the ground and found Caroline's will still in the lockbox. "Is it this?"

In front of my eyes, the edges of the paper began to burn. The old paper ignited into flames. I dropped it and stomped out the fire. The fragile pieces broke apart, but the flames were out.

"Are you trying to burn down Whitehall Manor?" I yelled as I bent down to pick up the journal.

The journal burned in my hands. "I know who you are," I said.

The pages flew open. The writing was manic. Words crisscrossed the pages. My eyes flashed to vulgar scenarios. Pornographic drawings were scattered from page to page. The pages stopped on a dark figure with red, beady eyes. It stayed there for a moment as my eyes took in the meaning. Somehow evil had returned to Whitehall Manor. My stomach turned but I couldn't let go of the journal.

"Leave me alone," I begged as tears welled in my eyes, but it was no use. Something controlled me at that moment. It had worked into my head and forced me to look.

The sketched drawings continued. Armies of insects crawling from a man's head. A woman being tortured, her hands held behind her back. Skeletal babies were torn limb from limb. Then, his eyes again. His sharp wicked gaze burrowed into mine.

At that moment when J.B. Towry took hold of me, I felt as if I'd been thrown into a deep dark well, forever lost to the Towry curse. The pages flew again stopping on a passage written in manic handwriting. There was only one way to get away from the grip that possessed me. I had to read it if I wanted to get out.

CHAPTER
NINE

You wanted to know about the curse? That was your first mistake. Your curiosity led you to this moment. They say to never ask questions if you don't want to know the answers. You've asked and now you will hear the truth.

You guessed correctly that I am John Burton Towry, the rightful owner of Whitehall Manor. I was born in November of 1838. My parents died from Yellow Fever when I was twenty-one leaving my sister, Caroline, in charge of Whitehall Manor.

The mistake of leaving the inheritance to my sister was what led to her downfall. There have been others who have tried to lay claim to Whitehall Manor since then. All of whom suffered dearly until they relented. Don't think for a moment that you will be any different.

Those gardens you adore will be torn asunder.

Your affection for the land will turn to misery.

All that you love will suffer unspeakable torture.

You are powerless to stop me, so do not try. Others have tried and failed. They've suffered for their attempts.

I know your thoughts. I watch you when you sleep and know your weaknesses. You are stubborn like a Towry and hopeful like

61

that woman named Seraphine who couldn't survive the curse no matter how hard she tried. It took decades but I worked on the weakest minds and turned them against her. I laughed when she met her tragic ending. I will laugh when you meet yours. I will rejoice when I take and mutilate your unborn child as I did with the others.

I've killed before. Nine children to be exact. They were my sister Caroline's children born beneath the ground where I put her. Each time she gave birth, I made sure to mutilate their corpses, sometimes throwing them into the field for the hawks to eat. Other times, I drowned them in Willow Creek. Some were born dead, too terrified to face what waited for them in this world. Others fought for survival but met swift deaths.

I will come for your child, too, Anne Towry, and drown it in the creek like the others if you don't leave Whitehall Manor. I will torture your every waking moment and those who decide to step foot on this land that is mine. Everything you build, I will tear down. Everything you love, I will kill. Everything you hope for, I will destroy.

No one owns Whitehall Manor but me, remember that. Leave now. This is your final warning.

-J.B. Towry

CHAPTER

TEN

"Shake her again," a voice said. "No, that doesn't work. Get some cold water. Call the doctor. Anne? Anne, please wake up. Anne?" A low and worried voice different from the one I had heard a moment ago broke through my thoughts.

From somewhere in my head, I could feel my sockets push the whites of my eyes back to level. The person before me was a blur and then came into focus.

Terran stared at me in horror. Behind him, Penelope was a blur.

Could he see the ghost? Could he hear the whispers as I could? Did he know that J.B. Towry forced me to take the journal from the cabinet and read his torturous deeds and violent threats?

I followed his gaze down to my shirt and saw his look had nothing to do with J.B. Towry. It was something else entirely. I was covered in my own blood. My hands began to tremble. The journal fell to the floor.

"Oh, god, Anne!" Penelope pressed a hand to her mouth.

There was no doubt the blood had started from my scalp again. I touched the wound and saw the bright red fluid on my fingertips.

"Let's get her out of the attic," Terran said to Penelope.

"It's not that bad," I said. "It's a surface wound. It looks worse than it is." I tasted a trickle of blood on my lip and the saltiness on my tongue. The smell of smoke lingered in the air. "Do you smell that?"

Terran shifted my arm as he helped me down the stairs. Penelope followed. It was dark now, pitch-black, and inside the house the hallway felt like an endless tunnel of flickering lights and smoke.

"He's following us," I said, glancing back. "Penelope, close the attic door. Don't go up there. Under no circumstances should anyone go up there."

She nodded. Her eyes tearing as she turned and rushed back to secure the door closed.

Once back in the sitting room, I saw the fire had nearly gone out.

"Get the First-Aid kit," Terran said to Penelope as she hurried from the room and he lowered me to the chair.

"You have to start the fire," I said to him.

"Not now."

"No, it must be now. We must start the fire, please."

He sighed and grabbed a few logs, stoking them until they smoldered.

Penelope returned. Her face was paler than normal. "Should I call the doctor?" she asked Terran, handing him the kit.

"No," I said. "I just didn't apply pressure for long enough. Please, keep the fire going."

Terran nodded to Penelope to do what I said, and the

housekeeper quickly worked on layering the wood into the hearth.

"Were you in the attic?" I asked her.

Penelope's eyes widened. "No. I was in my room."

"During the storm?" I asked.

"Yes."

"I called to you when I came inside."

"I didn't hear a thing except for the thunder. I'm sorry, Anne. I should have waited for you in the sitting room. I knew once the storm started, you'd be soaked when you came in."

I didn't like being neglected, but I hated being lied to. Penelope was always on the ball. Why had she ignored my calls? Pressing my lips together, I held back my reprimands. I didn't want Terran to see me at my worst again.

"Is there anything else I can do for you?" she asked.

I shook my head and Terran said, "You should go."

She slipped from the room leaving Terran and I alone again.

I took the towel and held it to the wound.

"It would make us all feel a lot better if you'd let me take you to the hospital," Terran said.

"No," I said, lowering my voice. "I'm not leaving my home." The thought of stepping foot off the property with J.B. Towry lurking in the attic whispering *My house* was out of the question. This was my battle, and I would end it one way or another.

"What happened up there?" Terran asked.

I shivered thinking about it then said, "It started in the cemetery when I was burying the bones. I was attacked."

Terran's fists clenched. "Who attacked you?"

"Not a person. A hawk. There must have been a nest

nearby. I couldn't see it but there wasn't a lot of time to look, not with the storm that started."

"Then how did you get from the garden to the attic with that wound? I don't understand. Start at the beginning. Tell me everything."

"I don't think that's a good idea."

"What do you mean? What's going on?" He stood back. "What are you hiding?"

I didn't like the anger in his voice. It rattled me. Even worse, it confused me. I didn't know where to start. Every bone in my body felt ice-cold. My lips, chapped and raw, made me think I'd lost oxygen to my brain. Had I held my breath in shock? Had I forgotten to breathe? The thought that a ghost could take my breath made me curl inward. He could take my life at any moment. I shook away my physical worries. My hands went to my stomach. This wasn't just about me. It was about my child. I wrung the cloth and turned toward the fire.

"Something's not right." Terran began to pace. "I saw the attic door open and went up there to see you standing by the wardrobe in the alcove covered in blood. Anne, I was so worried." He came to my side and kneeled. "You were mumbling words. Your eyes were rolled into your head. You were holding this journal. There was blood covering your face. Something's going on," he said, examining me. "You don't look like yourself."

"I nearly passed out in the shower."

"That's it. We're going to the doctor."

"No."

"Why are you so stubborn?"

I wanted to tell him what had happened in the attic. I needed to tell him about the haunting but couldn't. I couldn't even share with him the news about my pregnancy. Not yet. Something was holding me back from revealing everything to him. I held his hands. Red stains from my blood made my pale hands look pink. "So much happened to us only months ago. I want to move forward but I'm scared to."

He squared his shoulders. "Tell me what happened in the attic."

Pulling away, I turned toward the fire. It was impossible to explain. I didn't want to frighten him. What could Terran do anyway? If there was a ghost, one that demanded we leave, he would think I was crazy, or worse he would try to force me to leave with him and I couldn't. I couldn't relinquish control of Whitehall Manor and let it slip back into its haunted state. No, I would keep my thoughts to myself.

"If you can't open up to me, then we have nothing," Terran said.

"Please, give me some time to sort things out. All the changes. My new role as the head of this home. Losing my parents. The upcoming charity event. There's so much to think about. I don't know if what I'm experiencing is real or not."

"You can't keep all of it to yourself. Don't you remember that's what your father did? He hoarded to keep himself safe and not from Maura Wells' ghost but from himself."

"My father was sick," I said. "He was very sick. He was disturbed and schizophrenic. He had the Towry curse."

"There's no curse."

"There is," I said, remembering the words I read in Caroline's will. She knew her brother was sick, demented is what she wrote, but she was powerless to stop his crimes. "There's something passed down, something genetic. I don't know all the information. I know that it's still here at Whitehall Manor."

Terran stared at me. He scratched his jaw before letting his hands fall to his sides. "If you think that, then why are we here?"

"It's worth fighting for," I said. "We love Whitehall Manor. This is our home."

"It's your home," he said.

I fought back tears. "Don't say that." I faced the fire feeling hopeless. I was on the brink of losing the man I loved, the father to my child, and possibly my mind, but I couldn't give in. I had to figure out a way to keep Whitehall Manor and the baby safe.

Before I could say anything else, Terran turned to leave.

The stillness of the house sank into me, and I was brought back to the days when I first arrived. I gazed into the burning fire, mesmerized by the heat, and listened more closely to the whispers. There was something the house wanted to tell me. After a few minutes, I heard the words and again felt a chill race down my spine. J.B. Towry was here. He was everywhere. He was listening. My god, this was too big for me to handle alone. I thought of Salazar's words. I needed Terran.

"Terran," I called out.

His footsteps returned to my side. His hands were on my face. I was embracing him tightly. His warmth and that of the fire strengthened me.

"Please, don't go. Don't leave me alone. I need you."

"Tell me what's frightening you."

"I will," I said, drying my cheeks. "The journal. It belonged to J.B. Towry. I went to the attic yesterday to look for items for the auction and found it. I didn't even mean to.

It fell from a shelf. When I first read it, I felt horrible, like something was working its way into me. Something wicked. Oh, it was wicked. The things he wrote would turn anyone sick."

"Where is the journal now?"

"It's still up there. In the attic."

"I'll get it and throw it in the fire."

"Yes, you must. You must get rid of it. We must get rid of his ghost from this house. If we don't, he won't stop. He will come for us. He hates children. He hates anyone who could lay claim to the house. First, he will try to kill me, and then—"

Terran gripped my hands tightly in his. "Anne, stop it. Stop it! This is all in your head. There's no ghost."

"There is. I know it. What's worse is that J.B. Towry has done this before. He's worked his way into people's heads and manipulated them to do terrible things."

He stared at me dumbfounded and then said, "If you want to leave Whitehall Manor today, I will leave with you. I won't leave you alone, but you have to let this go. It's all in your head. Please. If you don't, you'll go crazy. Please, Anne." Tears glistened in his blue eyes. "Do it for us. Give our future a chance."

"That's what I'm trying to do," I whimpered.

He held me again. The soft sound of his heartbeat comforted me. How had I ever distrusted Terran? He was always running to my rescue, and I was always doubting him.

"You need rest. Let me take you to bed."

"No, not yet," I said, taking a breath. "There's one more thing I need to tell you." How I loved Terran. I wanted to be his wife. I wanted us to live together forever at Whitehall

Manor, in our secret home far away from the rest of the world. I wanted to return his promise of hope and put aside my fears so that we and Whitehall Manor could have a future and to do that I had to trust him. I had to do whatever it took to fight against my fears.

"Terran," I said, holding his hands. "I'm pregnant."

PART TWO
MAY

ELEVEN

"The guest list is finalized," Penelope said, handing it to me.

I shifted in Father's chair. His office had been remodeled slightly to my liking. Gone were the blackened lanterns, outdated bookshelves, and old-fashioned windows. Everything was modern and fitting for a shore house. I scanned through the names and recognized several society locals. "And we have all the items ready to sell?"

"Yes, everything is ready."

I tapped a pencil to my lip. "In two days, the caterers arrive. The musicians set up before noon. We have enough canapés to feed three hundred. What else am I forgetting?"

Penelope smiled and refilled my teacup. "Your gown?"

"Yes, I'll wear the only one that fits me now. The blue one with the pearls."

"You'll look lovely no matter what you wear."

She was still sweet as ever despite the additional duties I placed on her to-do list. Most of the charity event was what she put together. I stood and went to the window. Gazing out to the gazebo in the back of the house with tables and chairs set up for the lunch, I felt reassured that for the first time, Whitehall Manor would finally shine as it was meant to.

"How about something simple for dinner?" Penelope asked.

"Yes, something simple is fine."

I hated to pretend I wasn't famished all the time. I could eat a two-pound steak if it was put in front of me right now. I was now five months into my pregnancy and craving just about everything. The glow from two months ago had long since worn off leaving me with the beginnings of an achy back and swollen feet. I spent most of my mornings in the orangery feasting on Salazar's fruits, stripping whole trees bare of their lush oranges and bananas. The ripened cherries didn't stand a chance. I devoured them by the fistful. And, as promised, I ate Salazar's famous broth at lunch every day and felt my hair grow thicker along with my waistline.

Closing the accounting book, I tucked it back into the drawer and then opened the one beneath it to find a few candies that I kept there now like Father had. I couldn't help but get excited about my child one day sitting on my lap and finding the secret stash.

It had been two months since the incident in the attic. Terran and I didn't speak of it. I knew it had been something in J.B. Towry's journal that triggered the break. Once Terran burned the journal, the nightmares stopped. I stayed out of the attic for fear of another encounter, but it seemed as long as Terran and I united forces and continued to move forward, nothing, not even a ghost from the eighteen hundreds had any power over us.

Thinking about the future made me want to check on the progress of the baby's room. I pushed away from the desk and worked my way past a few maids busily cleaning the floors and polishing the banisters to the other end of the house and up the stairs to the room that Terran joyfully gave up and had since been transformed into the baby's room.

The door was framed, the old yellow wallpaper removed, a fresh color of neutral paint applied, and best of all, the original flooring glistened from a recent polishing. I leaned close to the window and let my mind wander to how far I'd come. Only a few months ago I was alone, more alone than anyone could be, and so quickly my whole life changed.

Terran, Whitehall Manor, the money, and now the baby. Soon, the house would be filled with sounds of laughter and the pitter-patter of feet rushing down the hallways. The more I thought of it, the more I realized that whatever lurked in the attic two months ago was gone, forced out by the positive brilliance of hope and determination.

I sighed wondering if the baby would be a boy or a girl.

Outside the window, I couldn't help but notice something staring back at me. In the tree was a hawk sitting on a branch that extended outside the window. It was barely noticeable as it blended in with the leaves except for its beady red eyes that stared through the glass as if it were staring at me.

I ran a nervous hand through my hair. I would not let my fears take hold of me again. Terran had made it clear. It was our future together or the past alone. The decision was obvious. I needed Terran. Whitehall Manor would thrive and to do so meant pushing out the nightmares, forgetting the fears, and ignoring the signs that J.B. Towry still lurked the hallways.

Despite the whispers in my ear, even the ones I could hear right now, telling me the house was his, that he would come for my child, that he would destroy everything I built, I persevered, ignoring the wicked thoughts.

"Get away," I said to the hawk. "This is my nest. You won't come in here."

The bird lifted from the branch and took flight.

I craned my neck to see it fly toward the cemetery and couldn't help but wonder if it was the same bird that attacked me.

"So, what do you think?" Terran asked.

I turned to see him behind me. "I love it," I said. "It's close enough to our room that we can be here quickly for nighttime feedings but far enough that we can still have our privacy."

He leaned closer and kissed me. His warm lips ignited my passion. The spark was there but strangely I recognized a hint of something else flowery.

"Have you been working in the orangery?" I asked.

"You know I'm not allowed in there," he said. "Not since your grandfather told me he was in charge of the citrus growing at Whitehall Manor."

"You smell like—"

"Oranges?" he said, producing two fresh ones, one from each pocket.

"Oh, they look delicious." I grabbed one, sat in the rocking chair, and began peeling it. "Did you see Penelope on the way up?" I asked.

"Yes, why?"

"I was wondering if she showed you the list for tomorrow. There will be over three hundred people here."

"We knew the event would have a huge turnout. Are you nervous?"

"I suppose. I want everything to go right."

"Everything will be fine," he said, kissing my forehead. "You leave the worrying to me."

"And what should I do?"

"Bring your beautiful self."

"Oh, I don't know about that. Have you seen my ankles?"

"I love your ankles?"

I laughed and kissed him once again.

"I'm heading into town to get a few last-minute things. Need anything?"

"A steak," I said before I could stop myself. "A huge steak, as big as you can find."

He saluted me and I laughed as I tore apart the orange and sank my teeth into it.

Once Terran was gone, I stared down at the gazebo below where the staff worked to tie the last few ribbons on chairs. They bustled around setting up centerpieces while the gardeners finished the last of the tree-trimming and skimmed the pool.

A voice pushed into my ear. "*Get out.*"

I ignored the noise and continued to eat my orange.

The room was silent for a moment, then suddenly the chair rocked me to the floor. I slammed to my side. The second orange tumbled to the corner. A sharp pain pulsed in my hip. I moaned in agony. I slowly pulled myself up and stared at the chair. It stopped rocking just as quickly as it had started.

I wouldn't let him get the best of me. I fled from the baby's room and pulled the door closed. It would do little to contain J.B. Towry and his threats. He roamed free throughout the house, but I had another idea. One that would hit him where it hurt.

"Everything okay?" Penelope asked me as she directed a few of the staff through the hallway.

"Yes," I said, tucking the half-eaten orange into my pocket.

"Oh, those are lovely, aren't they?" she said.

My eyes went to where she was looking. "The oranges are Salazar's specialty," I said.

"Yes, I had one myself this morning." She hurried the last of the staff out of the master bedroom. "Rooms are clean now. Would you like me to turn down your bed for a nap?"

"No, there's no time for that," I said. "I'd like to go through the items for the auction one more time. Then, the staff will need to set them up in the orangery."

"Of course," she said. "Anything else?"

"Yes," I said. "A redtail hawk is lingering by the window of the baby's room. I believe it's the same one that attacked me. Tell me the head gardener I want it shot. Bring the dead bird to me once it's been done."

Penelope's eyes grew larger. "Shot? A red-tailed hawk? Forgive me, but I think they are protected birds. You could get in trouble for killing one."

"This is my home," I said, walking past her. "I will do as I please. Tell the gardener I want the bird dead and if he won't do it, I will."

CHAPTER

TWELVE

Most of the items for the auction had been brought into the orangery and lay on tables beside the podium. It would take all afternoon to auction off the bulk of what we had collected.

Salazar did his best to relent some of the entertainment space, only mildly objecting when I told him he'd have to move his saplings to the far end of the building.

In addition to the dresses, wigs, sculptures, and figures, there were a few scrolls of paper that listed the land rights purchased by the early settlers, the house design in later years, and three early black and white photographs of the home.

"I should get the original house plans to the local archives," I said to Penelope as she set up the auction area with the microphone and gavel.

"Why not wait until after the party?" she said.

"There's nothing else to do. You've taken care of all the planning. No, I don't want to sit around idly until tomorrow."

"That's a good idea," she said. "Besides, I don't think

you've left Whitehall Manor in weeks. It will be good to get out for a few hours."

"Agreed," I said, looking through the plans for the original ones. Once I had them, I waved and headed toward my car.

Penelope had been right. It had been weeks since I sat in my car. My belly was too close to the steering wheel now. I shifted the car seat back giving myself a few inches of space and then started the car.

A few miles down the long dusty road, past full and billowing trees and fields full of spring crops, I came to the main road that led to Ashbury. It was nice to get out. The afternoon air was fresh and mild, perfect for the month of May. Every morning there appeared another litter of animals born in the night. The green lush leaves of the oak trees flourished again in the light. The air smelled clean with the hint of perfumed flowers. Whitehall Manor was too important to leave. I knew I'd fight for it. No matter what it took.

A car passed and I gazed into the passenger's face not recognizing them but feeling suddenly strange. It dawned on me that my world had become too small at Whitehall Manor. My daily routines were too predictable. My worries, too consistent. Getting out was good for me. The party would be even better.

I turned left and headed five miles into town and toward the local archives. A few minutes later I pulled into their parking lot and walked carefully toward the front door. The sting in my hip from being hurled to the ground from the rocking chair kept me from going as fast as I wanted. I couldn't help but wonder if this would be the way of things for the next few months. I dreaded the thought of not being able to physically do what I could only a few months ago but there was no sense in agonizing over it. The pain was worth it. In a few months, I'd have my child in my arms. I felt my heart skip a beat as I realized I was more than halfway there.

Pushing open the front door to the archives, I turned to see an empty desk with no one behind it. I glanced at the time. I wasn't too late, was I? I knew they were only open a few hours each week. I scanned the room for someone who could take the house plans from me.

The archives were located in an old dancehall that had been used by the women of Ashbury for their meetings and charity events. Now, the stage at the far end of the room had what looked like a shipbuilding display, and around the room were various paintings, photographs, and maps, showing off the area's oldest homes, monuments, and events. A local school teacher had created a timeline of events that led to Ashbury's inception. Beside the desk was a photograph of a celebrity who had come to visit and signed his headshot with the words, *Love your crabs*.

"Hello," a woman with short, blue-gray hair and a friendly smile said. She emerged from the stage where she had been propping up a display of eighteenth-century canning techniques.

"Oh, hello," I said, slowly approaching her. "I've come to drop off these house plans. They are the original plans to Whitehall Manor that I promised to bring."

"Oh, yes. You must be Ms. Towry."

"Yes, I'm Anne Towry." I handed over the plans and she took the rolled-up paper and slowly unrolled it onto the desk.

She introduced herself as Mabel Lindstrom. Her hands were thick with blue veins. I spotted a smudge on her oversized glasses. The scent of something medicinal lingered in the air.

"It's most generous of you to donate these to the archives," she said.

"It's the least I can do. I have other things that are to be auctioned tomorrow at Whitehall Manor's charity event. Will you be there?"

"Oh, yes, I wouldn't miss it. Whitehall Manor has always been a deep fascination of mine." She gazed at the house plans for a moment. "I'll have these mounted on the wall. So many visitors will be fascinated by the architectural style and design."

"I'm hoping everything will be sold at tomorrow's auction. We'll be donating the money we make to Ashbury's community center, but what doesn't sell I could bring here. I may have a few other things to donate. Dresses, wigs—"

"Oh, that's kind of you but we mostly collect records, photographs, maps, and such."

I scanned the room and saw an old picture hanging on the wall of Whitehall Manor. "Is that—?"

"Yes, that's a photograph of Whitehall Manor from the nineteen hundreds."

I went to it and examined the photograph recognizing the familiar pillars and whitewashed exterior, even the cross windows that extended from the east to west wings. The window to the baby's room was concealed. As I reached out to touch it, I said, "Oh, I've never seen it like this before." My gaze fell on the man standing in the gravel driveway. "Who is this?"

The woman fixed her glasses and looked closely. "Well, that's Thomas Towry. He would be your—"

"Great grandfather," I said. I looked at his serious gaze.

He had a jawline like my father and steely eyes that stared straight at the camera and felt like he was staring straight at me. So, this was Caroline's son who inherited Whitehall Manor after she died. "You don't by chance have any other photos, do you?"

She shuffled over to a cabinet and went through several files until she found one that said Whitehall Manor and pulled it out. Together we sat at her desk as she pulled everything she had out of the envelopes tucked into the file.

There were a few more photographs of Thomas in a sailboat and one of a child who must have been my grandfather. It felt like I was gazing through time. "Oh, they look so happy," I said. "And Whitehall Manor looks magnificent."

"It's always been a spectacular property," she said, reaching into the file. She pulled out another photograph and laid it in front of me. I pulled back feeling suddenly stricken with panic.

"W-what is this?" I asked, my voice feeling weaker.

"This would be your great-great-grandfather, J.B. Towry."

"No, that's wrong." I looked at his face distorted with madness. He gazed at the camera. The image was a daguerreotype with faded edges. In his eye was an evil and mystical glare, clouded by a half smile that looked nothing else than wicked. "J.B. Towry was my uncle."

The woman reached into the envelope again and laid out a photograph of a woman with long smooth blond hair and crystal eyes. Before she said anything, I knew it was Caroline.

"This is Thomas's mother, Caroline," I said, grabbing the picture. She looked to be around seventeen, young and fresh. Another daguerreotype. Despite the faded edges, it was clear to see she was a great beauty, well-deserving of multiple admirers.

The woman put the envelope down. She took the two photographs of J.B. Towry and Caroline and slid them together. "Yes, this is Thomas's mother." She tapped on Caroline's photo, then slid her finger to the image of J.B. Towry and tapped there. "And this was Thomas's father."

I felt my core disintegrate. "His uncle. Her brother." The journal entry flashed through my mind. She had given birth to ten children, nine of whom died at the hands of J.B. Towry.

My eyes searched the old woman's. "Are you saying what I think you're saying?"

"Oh, my." The woman lowered her gaze. "How do you not know what happened?"

"I came late to the game," I said. "My mother, Seraphine, sent me away from Whitehall Manor when I was a child. She sent me away to protect me from my father, but by the look of things, I think she protected me from much more."

"This is a newspaper from the day that Caroline Towry was rescued."

"Rescued?"

"Unfortunately, Whitehall Manor was the scene of an unspeakable crime in the late eighteen hundreds."

I pressed my nails into the palm of my hand. "Did it have to do with children?"

"So, you do know."

"Some of it," I whispered. I remembered the graphic passages I had read from J.B. Towry's journal. "His deep fascination with being the sole owner of Whitehall Manor took on new meaning. He had been willing to do whatever it took to kill anyone who got in the way."

The archivist sighed as she said, "Caroline Towry recounted the assaults to investigators. The poor woman must have had to give birth nine times alone in the cellar. How she survived all those years is beyond me."

My head spun. I steadied myself against the table. "What else do you know? How did this happen?" I could hear my voice stretching thin.

She reached into the envelope once more and placed another photograph in front of me. It was J.B. Towry in a wheelchair. His head was twisted to the side and his eyes stared to the ground. He was bone thin. His withered body looked skeletal and reminded me of Father in his last hours. He held a sign that read *Baltimore Sanatorium 1921*.

"Are there any records, medical records for him?"

"You'd have to go to Baltimore to get those."

"What else do you know?"

"From what I've been able to piece together, J.B. Towry had been expelled from WestPoint Academy after a particularly vicious duel in which he killed a fellow cadet."

"That doesn't surprise me."

"He was expelled and returned to Whitehall Manor to find out that he'd been disinherited. The fortune was left to his sister, Caroline."

"Then his parents died," I said, reciting everything I remembered from his journal.

"Correct. Yellow Fever spread like wildfire in 1859 throughout the major cities and even into small towns like Ashbury. His parents both contracted the disease and died. Their deaths must have pushed J.B. Towry to the edge."

I didn't dare say what I felt, which was that he had more than likely been born over the edge, long before he killed a fellow cadet or the death of his parents.

After taking a deep breath, the woman went on. "Unfortunately, J.B. Towry held his sister captive in a root cellar on Whitehall's property. He told the locals that she had married a suitor in San Francisco. Some of her childhood friends tried to find her but couldn't. There was no proof that she hadn't moved out west. After a while, people gave up looking. The property rights never changed, but J.B. Towry continued to live at Whitehall Manor for the next twenty years."

My hands shook and I placed them in my lap. "Caroline was eventually found. Tell me what happened to her."

"After twenty-one years they found her barely clinging to life. She was eighteen when he held her against her will. She was nearly forty years old when she was found. You can read the newspaper clipping to see. It must have been traumatic for her. She was discovered along the road to Ashbury, only a few miles from the manor home."

I cringed thinking of the torment she must have experienced. "How could she have survived for that long?"

"I don't know," the woman said. "Except she was strong and determined to see J.B. Towry held accountable for his crimes."

The woman across from me pushed forward the newspaper clippings.

With shaky hands, I picked them up and read.

THIRTEEN

Asbury — July 25, 1881

A woman identified as Caroline Towry, the legal owner of Whitehall Manor, has been discovered wandering the road, three miles outside of Ashbury, by a local farmer. Ms. Towry was discovered in tattered clothing and a state of confusion. She was discovered around dusk on July 23 and transported to the local hospital for care.

The physicians who treated Ms. Towry describe her condition as life-threatening. She weighs only seventy-five pounds, has obvious signs of trauma and scarring to her face and other regions of her body, and is reported to be seven months pregnant. As one physician states, "It is a miracle she's still alive."

Her prognosis for survival is unknown. There are no surviving members of the Towry family other than her brother, J.B. Towry, who investigators have not been able to discover at this time.

Ashbury — July 28, 1881

Mr. John Burton Towry, the brother of Ms. Caroline Towry,

has been arrested without incident at Whitehall Manor, discovered in an upstairs bedroom of the house. After his sister was found wandering the road to Ashbury only five days prior, she was able to tell investigators her brother had kept her locked in a root cellar following a disagreement over legal rights to the Towry fortune including property rights to Whitehall Manor. Ms. Towry was held against her will for over twenty years, surviving on scraps that Mr. Towry fed her and rainwater that dripped through the cellar door. She was found in a state of great malnutrition and is currently clinging to life. Everything is being done to try to keep her and her unborn child alive.

J.B. Towry was charged with kidnapping, assault, and rape of his sister, Ms. Caroline Towry. Further evidence provided by Caroline Towry suggests that murder will also be added to the list of charges as it is suggested by the local sheriff put in charge of investigating this matter that Caroline has given birth to nine children over the last twenty years, all of whom were either murdered or discarded on Whitehall Manor's property. Investigators have cordoned off the area in their search for evidence in this matter. Caroline Towry continues to battle for her life. J.B. Towry is being held in the local jail until a decision can be made as to his competency.

ASHBURY — *August 10, 1881*

Shocking news from Whitehall Manor where investigators have discovered the remains of two infants on the property. Two bodies were found in separate locations. Bones from one of the bodies were partially found while a second newborn body was unearthed in a nearby field. According to Ms. Caroline Towry, she claims to have given birth to nine children, all of whom she presumes are dead at the hands of her brother, J.B. Towry, who after a medical examination has been deemed incompetent to stand trial and will be institutionalized at the Baltimore Asylum for the Criminally Insane for a duration to be determined.

ASHBURY - SEPTEMBER 2, 1881

The child of Caroline Towry was born this morning. The owner of Whitehall Manor gave birth prematurely to a boy who she has named Thomas Towry and who is now in the care of Dorothea Barrow of Baltimore while Ms. Caroline Towry works toward recovery from the gruesome wounds she endured at the hands of what we now know is her demented and sadistic brother, J.B. Towry. Investigations continue at Whitehall Manor where detectives have now unearthed four corpses of infants. The remaining bodies are registered as missing and presumed to be decomposed at this time.

The infant, Thomas Towry, stands to inherit the mass of Whitehall Manor's fortune as reports from Ms. Towry's attorney state she is determined to make sure the property falls in the right hands and never into the control of J.B. Towry. With his institutionalization at Baltimore's Asylum for the Criminally Insane, there seems little chance of that ever happening.

I FINISHED the last of the newspaper clippings and slid them back toward the archivist. "Is this all there is about J.B Towry?"

"I'm afraid so," she said.

"So, the story ends with J.B. Towry being institutionalized?"

"I'm afraid Caroline died only a month after giving birth. Whitehall Manor remained unoccupied for eighteen years until her son, Thomas, was old enough to take over."

"Did they ever release J.B. Towry? Did he ever return to Whitehall Manor?"

"I'm afraid I don't know," she said.

She searched through the file and found one more article and laid it in front of me. The dates had jumped ahead and the newspaper font was different. I scanned the words.

November 2, 1923

Sad news once again from Whitehall Manor. The famed inheritor of the Whitehall Manor estate, Mr. Thomas Towry, has died.

After inheriting the mass of the Towry fortune when he turned eighteen, Mr. Towry seemed poised to erase his father's horrible legacy in which he imprisoned Thomas's mother in a root cellar for over twenty years. Thomas Towry married in 1911 and doubled his fortune within ten years through investments in oil and transportation. After traveling with his wife and son, George Towry, to Europe for an extended vacation, the family returned six months ago to Whitehall Manor.

The circumstances around his death are raising suspicions with local authorities who have been sent to the property to investigate. As for now, it appears Thomas Towry who was on top of his game chose to end his life for unknown reasons.

Reports say his body was found hanging from a rafter inside a toolshed on the property. His death is a shock and loss to our community as mourners line the gates of Whitehall Manor leaving flowers and sending condolences to his surviving wife and child who have reportedly left Whitehall Manor without any plans of returning.

Funeral details will be provided in the coming days.

· · ·

"I'M afraid I don't have anything else to share with you," the woman said, emptying the file. "I know how terrible it must be to read these things about your relatives. Murder, rape, and suicide. Not to mention the supposed hauntings going on over there and the most recent deaths."

"You mean my parents."

"Yes, my condolences."

I leaned in closer. "Do you believe the Towrys are cursed?"

"Now, don't say that." The woman tapped my hand. "Those are rumors. It's bad luck is all. Aren't things better now?"

"Yes."

"You will change the rumors."

"Yes, I had wanted to open Whitehall Manor to the public. That was the point of the charity event. Soon the renovations will be done, and everyone will be welcome there." I lifted my chin and smiled through glistening tears. "It's hard to have to be this strong all the time, you know?"

"Show them tomorrow that there is no curse."

I straightened my shoulders. "I will." I slowly stood and headed out of the local archives wondering if digging into my family history was wise. My promise to Terran was to leave it alone. I had managed for two months to control the thoughts and whispers. If only my curiosity didn't keep getting the best of me. I wiped tears from my cheeks and headed back to Whitehall Manor trying to shake the image of seeing Caroline wander the road I traveled half-alive, half-dressed, and seven months pregnant.

As I slowed to a stop outside Whitehall Manor, I stared ahead at the majestic property. If not for me, the house wouldn't have been restored to its original magnificence. The shimmering tree leaves, the lush lawn, and the stark white building against the red hues of a setting sun were all breathtaking. All this beauty was mine. I wouldn't run away afraid. I wouldn't let a maniac from the past try to terrify me. I was strong enough to endure anything.

Just then, the sound of a shotgun blast echoed around me. I smiled and smoothed a hand over my belly. The battle for Whitehall Manor was over.

FOURTEEN

The day of the charity event had arrived. The sky was blue, not a cloud in the sky.

Whitehall Manor had never looked so amazing. Every downstairs room was opened for guests to wander through, the provisions had arrived, and an extra ten staff members were brought on to prepare the food, while a team of waiters and bartenders were hired to make sure everyone was well taken care of during the event.

Best of all, the flowers in the Marigold Garden had blossomed creating a symphony of color that no one could say wasn't the absolute pinnacle of Whitehall Manor's beauty. The surrounding gardens, lawns, flowers, and trees had been trimmed to perfection. The orangery would be the site of the auction, a tropical oasis with orange and lemon trees and the scent of citrus mingled with the earthy scents of the rich soil Salazar used to cultivate his garden.

A space had been cleared for the items for auction. With the spring warmth and full sunshine of the last few days, everyone seemed to be in a festive mood.

Penelope fastened another pin into my hair.

I eyed her reflection in the mirror then turned to examine my royal blue dress and smoothed back a loose piece of hair.

"You're radiating."

I wish that was true. Just that morning I had looked at myself in the mirror and saw the sallow color in my skin and the hollowness of my cheeks. "I'm showing now. Can you see?"

"Barely," she said. "You'll probably be one of those first-time mothers who doesn't show until her last month."

"I wish it was more noticeable. I want people to know that Whitehall Manor is going to be filled with children, a happy place, nothing like the rumors."

"You should focus on yourself. Take in all the admiration and jealousy. You know everyone at the party will be wishing they were you."

"Do you think?"

"Yes, of course. You have a beautiful home, wealth beyond theirs, a child on the way, and a gorgeous husband."

I cringed at her comment. She turned before I could ask anything more.

"You need a little bit more rouge," she said, touching the brush to my cheekbones.

I knew Penelope didn't have children but as I looked at myself in the mirror and saw my pale, gaunt face looking back I had to ask her advice. "Is it normal to look so unwell during pregnancy?"

"Unwell? You look wonderful."

I pinched my cheeks knowing that wasn't true. Why was she lying to me? "Maybe after the party, I will see the doctor to make sure everything is okay."

"That's a great idea," she said, glancing at her watch. "The guests should be arriving any moment."

I nodded and slowly stood. "Let's make sure they feel welcome."

Penelope hurried downstairs while I held back to make sure the door to the baby's room was locked. Guests could wander freely but not to that room.

When that was done, I made my way to where the head gardener waited for me near the back door. In his hands was the dead red-tailed hawk. I sighed and thanked him, making him promise to get rid of the bird and not mention it to anyone. His timing was perfect. I would have no harbingers of ill will at my party.

Outside, the cars came exactly at two o'clock. The valets rushed to move the luxury vehicles to the field, while the waiters welcomed the guests with a signature cocktail, the most expensive champagne money could buy blended with raspberry liquor.

On the other side of the home, several boats had anchored in the deep water. Small boats ferried well-dressed passengers to the dock where more waiters stood with glasses of sparkling champagne.

"Welcome to Whitehall Manor," I said, greeting the first few couples.

We chit-chatted for a while until a line of cars circled the drive and I hurried to ask some of the gardeners to assist with moving them. Everyone needed to feel that Whitehall Manor was the highlight of the year, the best experience to remember, and I needed everyone to work harder to make that happen.

After reprimanding a waiter for smoking a cigarette along the side of the house, I quickly found Penelope. "Where are all the extra waiters?"

"They're passing the hors d'oeuvres."

"Some are taking breaks," I snapped. "The guests are arriving."

"I'll make sure they're working."

I smoothed back my hair searching for Terran. He had to be out in the Marigold Garden, but I couldn't possibly make my way across the front lawn with the heels I was wearing.

"Hello, Ms. Towry," a woman with short gray hair said.

I smiled and greeted Mrs. Sinclair recognizing her to be one of the biggest contributors in all of Ashbury. Her gardens were talked about far and wide.

"Mrs. Sinclair, so nice to see you. Thank you for coming."

"I wouldn't miss it," she said. "I've got my eye on that black and white photograph of Whitehall Manor's earliest gardens."

"Oh, yes. The gardens at Whitehall have always been extraordinary. Have you had a chance to tour them yet?"

"No, but I will. You know, my family has lived in these parts for a long time and Whitehall Manor has always been a topic of many conversations."

"All good I hope," I said, nervously laughing as I spotted a group of children arrive with their parents.

"Well, now, I can't say that. There have been too many stories about the Towrys to say it was all good, but I'm sure you know that."

"I hope you're not referring to my father," I said, suddenly changing my tone.

"Oh, no, dear. Everyone knows it was a great tragedy what happened to your father."

I pressed my lips together afraid I might say something to drive her away.

As a waiter passed, I grabbed two of the red fruity drinks and put one in her hand, and took a long drink from the other tasting alcohol on my lips realizing my mistake. "I shouldn't have done that," I said.

"Done what?" she asked.

"This is alcoholic."

"Yes, dear. It's a party. Have fun." She turned with her drink and wandered toward another group of people unaware that I was five months pregnant.

I put down the glass and turned to scan the crowd for Terran. More children went screaming past me. This was not supposed to be a children's event but how could I be irritated by them? The sounds of children laughing and playing were exactly what I had wanted. Why then was it making me so angry? I took a breath and shifted my gaze.

Detective Richards had arrived. He walked with his wife toward a waiter with a tray of mini quiche. I had never seen him in white pants and a Hawaiian shirt. He looked like he was heading on vacation. His wife however wore a beautiful emerald-green dress. Her hair was braided nicely and dangled over her shoulder.

"Hello, detective," I said, greeting him and his wife.

"You've outdone yourself," he said. "Really transformed Whitehall Manor into something I never thought possible."

I smiled. "It was my mother's dream for all of this. I just put it into action."

"The marigolds are lovely," his wife said. "Their smell reminds me of my grandmother."

"They say their scent attracts the dead." I stopped myself realizing how odd that sounded at a festive event.

Detective Richards raised a brow, and his wife laughed it off. "I suppose that's why they remind me of her. My grandmother's been dead for twenty years."

"Did you get a chance to bury those bones?" he asked.

My head swiveled from left to right. "Please, detective. Keep your voice down, but, yes, everything has been righted. There are no problems now."

Overhead, a screech echoed.

All three of us shielded our eyes and looked up.

"A red-tailed hawk," his wife said. "Oh, I love to watch them fly. Aren't they beautiful?"

"No. They're annoying. Please excuse me," I said, rubbing my brow as I worked away from the groups of people moving toward the tents behind the house. I stopped a waiter to find out where Penelope was.

He shrugged.

"Do you know when the auction will begin?" a man I'd never met asked.

"I believe after lunch." I hurried away from him and toward what appeared to be multiple children gathering around something.

When I came to their side, I saw they had made a circle around an injured rabbit. One of the boys poked it with a stick.

"Stop," I said, taking the stick from him. "Can't you see the animal is injured?"

"We were helping it along," the boy said.

Helping it along? It reminded me of what my mother wrote in her journal, how nature protects us through its corrections. Here were these little murderers only more than willing to usher the rabbit to its death. I only wished nature would carry away these children, drown them in the creek. I felt my face pale. How could I have thought that? I shook away the thoughts.

"What's wrong with you?" the boy asked.

"Nothing. Leave," I said. "Go find your parents or I will tell them what you've done to this rabbit."

The children laughed and ran away.

A moment later, Penelope was at my side. "Is everything okay?"

"No," I said. "Please go get the head gardener. This animal must be put out of its misery and tell him the hawk he killed wasn't the right one."

"The right one?"

"The hawk he needs to kill is the one that lingers outside the baby's window. How hard is that?"

The rabbit twitched and I felt suddenly sickened by watching it cling to life.

"Are you sure you want the gardener to kill it?" Penelope asked. "I think there's a veterinarian here."

"I know what's going on," I said to her, a flat tone in my voice.

"What?" Her doe-eyes widened.

A group of women in hats wandered nearby, close enough to hear our conversation, so I bit my tongue. "I'll talk to you later."

Penelope hurried away to find the gardener, while I scanned the green lawns for Terran. I knew she was interested in Terran. All the times she had laughed when he was in the room, saying he was gorgeous. And the nights when he didn't come to bed. Had he been with her? I couldn't let my worries get the best of me. Not now. I was so close to transforming Whitehall Manor's reputation.

The musicians began to play. The string quartet returned normalcy to my agitated mind and seemed to lure people to the tent where their charming tune syncopated with the elegance of the party. Several waiters began serving lunch.

Oh, where was Terran? I needed him to be with me, but he was nowhere to be found.

Another few townspeople commented on how lovely Whitehall Manor looked, exceptionally beautiful in the spring and fall one person said as he told of working the fields as a child when it was owned by my father.

There seemed to be a natural suspicion of the Towrys, and I was not excluded but the more I made the rounds, the more it seemed people accepted me. I felt a weight lift and sat down to eat lunch with a few women from Ashbury's gardening club.

Between bites of salmon and asparagus dressed in the lightest cream sauce, we discussed each one of the gardens on the property. It's strange to some people but I knew at that moment that Whitehall Manor had the power to transform people. I knew it reflected our true natures and it preserved them. I had forgotten that and gazed out to the water remembering the plans I had made with Terran to go on a sailing adventure this summer.

"Will you excuse me?" I said to the women. "I believe the auction is going to start soon. I'd like to make sure everything is ready."

First, I'd have to find Terran. I slipped off my heels and hurried toward the Marigold Garden. Several guests saw me and waved. One woman stopped me to say what a wonderful job I had done with Whitehall Manor. Only a few feet after that, a man stopped me to ask about hosting other events on the property, really opening it up to the community as I had promised.

"Oh, we'll have to see," I said. "We're still making the renovations."

"They're about to start the auction," one woman said.

"Yes, I'll be there in a moment."

Around the corner, I entered the boxwood maze and worked my way around the pathways to the end of the Marigold Garden. At the edge of the garden, I spotted Terran standing there with Penelope. She was leaning in, whispering something in his ear.

I clenched my fists. Was she trying to undermine my party?

She turned in time to catch my glare and hurried away as Terran began talking about the different types of hybrid flowers.

Suddenly, a bell sounded. I pressed my hands to my ears.

"The auction," Terran said, taking notice of me. "Excuse me," he said to the woman who was asking him about a particularly beautiful and rare pink marigold.

Terran came to my side. He reached for my hand and pulled me toward him.

"It's too much," I said. "All the people at Whitehall Manor. I can't breathe."

"You're fine," he said, pulling me gently to the corner and a quiet space with a stone bench. "Do you need some water?"

I shook my head. "Why are you doing this?"

"What?" he asked, searching my eyes.

This was hardly the time to confront him about his cheating. I was supposed to be in the orangery giving my speech, but I had seen them one too many times whispering to each other. Were they plotting something against me? Were they trying to undermine my success?

"What's going on?"

I stood feeling the grass on my bare feet and a sudden rebalancing of my center. I pressed the back of my hand to my head.

"I know you want to talk. You don't look yourself. What's going on?"

"I can't talk about it," I said. "Not now. Please help me to the orangery."

He did as I said and together, we walked out of the garden and back toward the house with several other pairs and groups of people who lingered in various spots of the fields taking pictures of the house.

All the doors to the orangery were wide open. Stepping inside felt less humid than usual. I spotted Salazar in the back and went to him.

"Your party is a success," he said.

"No," I said. "There's something wrong. I feel it in the air."

"Don't say that." Salazar led me around the corner past several people who lingered on the patio sipping drinks.

More children ran past, rattling me.

"I have to give a speech," I said, tears welling in my eyes. "Salazar, the house is haunted. I know it. I can feel J.B. Towry's presence."

His eyes searched mine. "Do you want the people to leave?"

I scanned the crowd. They were laughing and clinking glasses. Why couldn't I let my worries go? I knew why. My instincts were never wrong. I had followed them through every obstacle. "Yes," I said to Salazar. "I think that's best."

Terran overheard me and reached for my hand. He pulled me away from Salazar. "What are you doing?"

"He's here," I said.

"Stop it."

I swallowed.

"Get through the speech and then I'll take you inside."

Despite my nerves, I knew I had to face the community

and thank them for coming to Whitehall Manor. If I could only get through the next few minutes, I felt that everything else would be fine. I made my way to the podium where the auctioneer, an overweight man with a pink face and white hair, stood. He waited with the microphone.

With a shaky hand, I took it from him and turned to face the crowd. "Thank you for coming to Whitehall Manor today," I began.

The room grew silent except for the children outside and along the back. Each of the voices made me cringe and echoed in my head like tiny sirens.

"I wanted to say that I'm forever grateful that this community has supported me despite so many hardships. Whitehall Manor is a special and magical place, and I wanted you to see that for yourself. The auction today is for heirlooms from the Towry family and some of them date back to the early seventeen hundreds. All of the money that is raised today will be donated to Ashbury's community center."

The crowd clapped as I smiled and shifted my weight.

"I'm also pleased to say that the original designs for this home were donated to Ashbury's archives to be preserved for generations to come." My eyes fell on Mabel Lindstrom. The crowd clapped again. I swallowed and took a breath. "I have to thank all of my staff, my fiancé, and my grandfather for helping make Whitehall Manor return to what it was meant to be. I hope that in the coming months, we will be able to open the property for everyone to enjoy."

More cheers erupted with a few people shouting out they wanted to be first on the list to have their wedding near the waterfront. I smiled and relaxed. "Whitehall Manor has spent too much time being a home of secrets and mysteries and as you know we've also had our fair share of tragedies here."

I glanced out to the sea of faces. Everyone was so quiet. You could hear a pin drop. "But all of that has changed. Your being here today proves it. I've never seen such happy faces and enjoyed such wonderful conversations about the gardens." My eye fell on Salazar. "My mother would have been proud." I picked up the glass of water beside the podium and raised it. "To Whitehall Manor."

Everyone lifted their glasses and in unison said, "To Whitehall Manor" followed by more applause and smiling faces.

I gazed at Terran. His face beamed.

My moment had finally arrived. I was the lady of the manor, the official owner who had transformed a legacy of ill repute into something good. I had the power to do what generations before had struggled to do. I had righted the ship and steered the correct course to port.

"Well done," Terran said, hugging me.

The auctioneer wiped his brow and stepped up to the podium. "You've had a chance to look at everything and we will now begin the bidding."

A few moments later the first item, an eighteenth-century figurine was up for grabs. Paddles were raised as people fought to donate their money.

The sculptures were coveted by antique salespeople who upped their bids by hundreds of dollars at a time until finally the small figurine followed by two larger Romanesque items sold for thousands of dollars.

All the money would soon be in the hands of the community center. I pulled back my shoulders and smiled at the first row, Ashbury's elite. I had never been so proud.

Finally, both the Towrys and Whitehall Manor were back in the good graces of Ashbury's finest.

I refocused on the next item for auction, one of the black and white pictures. As the auctioneer did his best to ease into the bidding, my gaze fell on his assistant, a local boy who passed the items from the table to the auctioneer.

In his hands was a black book. My heart skipped a beat as I narrowed my gaze. He had the book open. Was it one of the first editions? I tried to maneuver closer to get a better view. The boy was reading the pages instead of paying attention to the auctioneer who had hit the gavel on the table and announced, "Sold!" to the highest bidder.

I snapped my fingers to get the boy's attention. When he looked up, I gasped, feeling the floor slip from beneath me. "No, no, no," I muttered. The whites of the boy's eyes were showing. His eyes had rolled back into his head.

"Terran." I grabbed his arm.

The auctioneer, clearly irritated by the boy's lack of attention, took the opened book from him and raised it above his head. It wasn't a book at all. My stomach twisted.

"The next item for auction is a leather-bound book which appears to be a record with notes from one of the Towry family, a Mr. John Burton Towry."

"The journal." I faced Terran. "J.B. Towry's journal. You said you burned it."

Terran's eyes darted to the auctioneer's hands. "I did."

Already several people had begun bidding. I gritted my teeth as the auctioneer flipped through the pages. Was he reading the words? His face paled. I grasped my necklace and chewed on my lip.

More people shouted out their bids, but the auctioneer had stopped talking.

"My god," I said. "He's reading the pages. You've got to get that journal."

Terran rushed to the front and snatched it from the auctioneer's hands. "This isn't up for grabs," he said.

I hurried forward but before I could say anything else, the auctioneer's assistant picked up the next item for bid, the cavalry sword.

He raised it level to the crowd and swung the blade.

Terran ducked in time, but the sword sliced through the air, cutting clear through the auctioneer's neck.

A splash of red blood doused the front row.

The crowd screamed.

I pressed a closed fist to my mouth as the auctioneer's head rolled to my feet.

Terran's eyes followed the man's body as it stood upright for several seconds spouting blood from the opening in its neck and then crumpled backward to the floor.

The boy took the sword and swung again in my direction.

"Anne!" Salazar yelled.

The blade came within centimeters of my skull. Before I knew what was happening, Salazar had pushed forward through a crowd of panicked guests toward my side. He helped me hurry away from the podium. Terran ran around the table joining the masses who were trying to fit through the door.

I turned back in time to see the boy pull the sword across his stomach. I held back horrified as the contents of his stomach spilled to the floor.

A woman beside me who had seen the same thing vomited.

Terran turned back to help the boy. I pulled away from Salazar and rushed to the front to help.

Blood trickled from both corners of the boy's mouth.

The panic continued as people rushed to the orangery's single exit, crowding into each other, causing more panic. A woman's face contorted as she gasped for air. Mrs. Sinclair fell to the ground, trampled on by several others. Ms. Lindstrom screamed out as she tumbled into one of the fountains. Detective Richards called for calm. Someone raised a chair and broke a window.

I rushed to grab the microphone while Terran held the dying boy.

"Please, everyone, calm down. Please, don't rush. Please."

It was useless. The yells turned to screams of terror. The shattered glass from the side of the orangery had cut into several people's faces. Small children cried in the corner, holding each other. Penelope was helped by Detective Richards who searched the crowd madly for his wife.

In a matter of minutes, the orangery was empty. Overturned chairs and tables lay scattered across the floor. Blood covered the floor. The items that had been sold at auction lay on the ground. Remnants of brochures, party napkins, plastic glasses, and half-eaten food scattered the tile. Injured victims who couldn't move called desperately for help while others lay unconscious.

Salazar stood in the back of the room, his eyes wide with horror at what had happened. I needed his comfort but before I could fall into his arms another scream erupted from outside.

Those who had not yet left the room and could move rushed outside to where a woman had been run over by a sports car peeling out of the driveway. Her body lay crushed beneath the still spinning tire, a splattering of brains and skull splashed along the drive that continued to be churned down to nothing under the wheel.

Around me, there were more screams until finally, people fled on foot down the drive, running to exit the gates, leaving their cars, belongings, and children behind.

In the pandemonium, I felt myself shatter. There was the Anne Towry of months ago, strong and determined, resilient against the odds, and there was the Anne Towry of this moment, shell-shocked into total disillusionment. How could I ever have thought Whitehall Manor could be anything other than what it was?

A whisper filled my head and when I turned, I looked up to the baby's room. To the room that I had locked and made sure no one could enter during the party. There, standing in the window was a shadowy figure watching me. I knew he was laughing. The sadistic bastard had successfully ruined everything.

CHAPTER

FIFTEEN

The next day following the charity event, I sat by the fire in the sitting room demanding Penelope put more logs on the fire. I couldn't shake the chill that had settled into my bones.

Terran tried to call the doctor, but I refused to be seen.

"Something haunts this home," I said. "It's doomed. No matter what we do, we are doomed."

"That's the past," he said. "You're thinking of your father and the past. What happened at the charity event didn't have anything to do with a haunting."

"No," I shook away his hand. If he didn't want to hear me, I had to accept that, but I knew the truth. "It's happening now. How else can you account for the boy killing the auctioneer and himself?" All I could see was the auctioneer's head rolling to a stop by my foot and the woman's skull pulverized beneath the tire of the car. And the boy's eyes had rolled up into his skull as mine had when I read from that journal. How could I forget his wicked smile before he cut open his stomach in front of the crowd, disemboweling himself in front of horror-stricken guests.

109

"The woman's death was an accident," Terran said.

"No."

"Then what?" Terran asked.

"I don't know."

"Anne, we've been over this a hundred times. The witnesses said the boy had been unstable. Some said they saw him talking to himself before grabbing the sword. His eyes had rolled into his head. Maybe it was a seizure. He snapped. We can't be held responsible for that."

"A seizure?" I laughed. "It was a possession."

I stared at him not sure how I could make him understand that occurrences like this at Whitehall Manor were never accidental. My mind flashed to the hours of chaos that followed the boy's death. The chaos that ensued. The poor mothers were screaming and clutching their children while guests tried in vain to make a call for emergency services, but the service to the property was never fully functional. I remembered feeling as if I was leaving my body as I clutched the leather-bound journal and screamed to the staff to get out. Blank and shocked faces stared back at me.

Penelope tried to pull me inside.

Terran finally succeeded and kept me in the east wing bedroom surrounded by the moaning and crying from outside. I was splattered in the child's blood and shaking uncontrollably. I stayed in that bedroom until finally the sun began to set, and the last of the injured victims, guests, emergency services, and staff had left.

Salazar and Penelope worked to clean up the mess. Why? I don't know except to say that they still had glimmers of hope that they could turn back the clock and fix something that was doomed. They should have left the glass and blood stains where they were and fled for their lives but no matter what I said to them, they wouldn't listen.

I walked at nightfall to the end of the drive, listening to the territorial calls of a robin and a distant scream of a red fox. As I came to the end of the driveway, I pulled the screeching iron gate closed.

I gazed out to the dirt road beyond Whitehall Manor knowing that my life was here now. I could no longer function in a world beyond Whitehall Manor. Whatever days remained would be here and knowing J.B. Towry and his will to possess the house, I knew my ending could be at any time. It didn't matter. I could never show my face in public again anyway. My life was effectively over.

Terran met me at the gate and led me back inside. It was too soon to talk but there was one thing I would do before the day ended.

Back in the sitting room, I walked to the fire and threw J.B. Towry's evil journal into the flames. Sparks flew up the chimney as I stoked the embers and watched the pages curl, lift in the heat, and burn to white-hot ash.

"None of this was your fault," Terran said, pulling me from my thoughts.

"Everyone will see that it is all a part of the Towry curse."

"There is no curse."

"How could you have not burned the journal as you promised?"

"I thought I did. It must have been a different book. I didn't know what exactly it looked like. You said a black leather-bound journal and that's what I burned."

"Clearly not," I said, trying to shift my tone. I didn't

want to fight with Terran, but we didn't see eye-to-eye on this matter. He didn't understand the stakes until it was too late, but I refused to let it go any further.

"What now?" he said, a dejected tone in his voice.

"I'm going to fix this," I said. "I'm going to get rid of J.B. Towry. He's here. Don't you see? He's haunting this house. He was in the orangery when he possessed that boy. He wants to make me suffer. Anything that brings me happiness he wants to take away. And the baby. Oh, Terran. He will take my baby."

"Stop it." Terran put his hands on my shoulders.

"Everything okay?" a voice said from the hallway.

We turned to see Detective Richards standing at the edge of the room. He eyed me, stepping closer. "Three deaths this year," he said. "Two deaths last year."

I knew what he was getting at.

Terran said, "We had nothing to do with the boy's death."

The detective fiddled with a figurine on the shelf. "What is it about Whitehall Manor that causes so many people to die here?"

It was the last thing I wanted to hear. I could barely keep myself together and the lingering feeling of a presence lurking nearby made the detective's visit unbearable. "You'll have to excuse me," I said. "I need to rest." I turned to leave the room.

"I heard you say J.B. Towry's name," he said.

I stopped in my tracks. "Have you heard his name before?"

Detective Richards worked his way across the room to the chair and sat. I slowly lowered myself to my chair while Terran hovered nearby.

"We've got records that go back a hundred or so years but not as far as when he was alive. All I know is that he may have been a rotten apple. Rotten to the core."

If only the detective knew what I knew. J.B. Towry was the rotten seed that cursed the Towrys' legacy.

"What do you want?" Terran asked the detective. "The investigation has been completed. There are hundreds of eyewitnesses. We can't be held responsible for the woman's death either. It was an accident."

He tipped his hat and was silent for a moment and then said, "In my limited experience with Whitehall Manor, I've learned one thing. One thing I know for sure."

"What's that?" I asked.

"When things get bad at Whitehall Manor, they're bound to get worse before long."

I swallowed, feeling he may be right. "The house is haunted," I said, a matter-of-fact tone in my voice.

"Anne." Terran held my shoulder.

I shrugged him off. "It's true. I saw J.B. Towry's face in the attic. Over the last two months, I've seen him in other places. I never said anything. I didn't want you to think I'm losing my mind. Rest assured, I'm not. I know what I saw."

Behind me, I could feel Terran turn away. It didn't matter. I needed allies and I was willing to tell the detective everything if it meant he would help me.

"I've seen him before looking down from my bedroom at me in the garden. Even when I'm swimming in the pool, I've looked back at the house to see his figure. He's a horrible man. Evil. Somehow, he's found a way to haunt Whitehall Manor. I thought it was through his journal but it's not. I feel his presence in the room now."

The detective sat up and looked around.

"Detective Richards, will you help me get rid of his ghost?"

"It's not exactly my area of expertise," he said.

Terran groaned. "Anne, please stop."

"No," I said. "Unless you can tell me that the boy who killed himself had been suicidal before his arrival to White-hall Manor, I'll go on believing he was possessed by that journal."

"Where's the journal now?" the detective asked.

"Burned," I said. "But there's something else of his still here that must be removed."

"What's that?"

"His body."

Terran shot from around the back of my chair to stare at me head-on. "This is insanity."

"Detective, I want the body of J.B. Towry exhumed from the Towry cemetery and buried somewhere else, a pauper's grave, or cremated, I don't care, but any sign of him needs to be off this property entirely. It's the only way to rid his connection to the land."

The detective glanced at Terran and then back at me. "You think that is what's going to fix all your problems at Whitehall Manor?"

"I know it's a start. I know that if my family is cursed, it's because of him and his actions. He committed crimes here. The body of the baby you found was his child, the child he made with his sister, Caroline Towry who he held prisoner in a root cellar that's since been filled in and destroyed."

"Anne?" Terran again pressed on my shoulder.

I shook it off. "Tell me, detective. Was the boy suicidal before he came to Whitehall?"

"No," he said. "His mother said he sang in the church choir. Never a sign of cruelty toward himself or anyone else his whole life."

"There," I said. "J.B. Towry wanted to put on a show. He got it. He ruined everything to try and take away my hope. He's trying to drive us away."

Detective Richards scratched his chin. "I've dealt with a lot of hauntings back in the city but never a possession."

Terran laughed. "You're not buying into this, are you? You're a detective. You're supposed to decide things based on facts."

"The facts are that we've got three dead people, one an accident, but the boy ..." He shook his head. "I can't make sense of it."

"Detective, I don't want to tell you any of this. I don't want to believe it myself, but it's the truth and I know because J.B. Towry wrote about his crimes in the journal that I burned. He must have enjoyed reliving his cruel acts by writing about them. He must have enjoyed every moment of the chaos yesterday. If we don't remove him from this property, he won't stop."

For the next few minutes, I told Terran and the detective everything I knew about the events that took place at Whitehall Manor from 1860-1881. I told them how the manor home was to be left in its entirety to Caroline. J.B. didn't agree with that and imprisoned her in the cellar out by the well in the garden. He tortured her there for twenty-one years. Caroline escaped and told doctors she gave birth to nine children while imprisoned. Four bodies were discovered. The other bodies must have been eaten by animals or thrown in the creek. We discovered the ninth body.

"Why are you telling me all this?"

"I-I'm telling you because you were the one who said there was a legacy of criminal insanity that ran in the Towry blood. It started with this J.B. Towry and I believe anything that continues to happen at Whitehall Manor will continue to happen until his body is removed."

"It's the past, Anne," Terran said. "He can't do anything to us."

"There is no past," I said. "The past never dies, but we can alter its course. We can protect ourselves and not run and hide from this."

Terran took a breath. He ran a hand through his hair.

I knew I had pushed him as far as he was willing to go, but I needed him to go a little further. I needed him to believe and trust me.

The detective eyed me suspiciously. After a few moments of silence, he said, "I came here tonight to tell you there wouldn't be an investigation into the boy's death, at least not here. We know you had no connection to him or the woman who died in the driveway."

I nodded but still felt the weight on my shoulders.

"You've got a problem," the detective said as he stood to leave. His eyes shifted to Terran. "A big problem that may not go away any time soon."

"Will you help us?" I begged.

"I don't know if I believe everything about the haunting, Anne, but it's your property, and if you want to dig up your long-dead ancestors, I can't stop you from doing it."

Terran shook his head. "Will digging up this body and getting rid of it put an end to this madness?"

I knew by the tone of his voice that he meant my madness, but it didn't matter. "Yes," I said. "I think it will."

"Fine. I have a buddy who can lend us a backhoe."

I sighed and went to Terran, pressing my hands to his chest. "Thank you" then turned and escorted the detective to the door. He headed out toward his car, disappearing into the darkness.

"Tomorrow morning," I said aloud to J.B. Towry. "Tomorrow, you leave Whitehall Manor for good."

CHAPTER
SIXTEEN

At dawn, the bulldozer came barreling down the lane along with Detective Richards driving a safe distance behind. The previous night's late-May rain had dampened the earth near J.B. Towry's grave and made it as soft as butter for the machine to cut through.

Terran gripped my hand as we stood near the gate. "Are you sure you want to do this?"

I turned and pressed a hand to his chest. "When you asked me to marry you, I'm sure you never thought this would be part of the plan."

His lips brushed against mine. "I wouldn't have asked you to marry me if I didn't know exactly what I was signing up for."

"Then trust me," I said.

He sighed and kissed me again as the man driving the backhoe stepped down from where he sat. "Which grave are we digging up?" he asked.

I separated from Terran and made my way into the cemetery, to the corner where J.B. Towry's crooked headstone was barely visible beneath the overgrown limbs of the willow tree beside it. "Let's cut these limbs back," I said to Terran who came with heavy clippers and cut them one by one until finally I could see the entirety of his tombstone.

John Burton Towry
1838-1921
"May God have mercy on your soul."

A shiver coursed through me. Not because of what I knew to be true about J.B. Towry, how he was pure evil, had tortured and impregnated his own sister, then killed their children, scattering their bodies throughout Whitehall Manor, but also that he lived for so long afterward.

I added up the years. He lived to eighty-three. He'd been found guilty of his crimes in 1881 at the age of forty-three but lived for forty more years in his insanity. How the doctors and nurses treated him once he was institutionalized was none of my concern. I hoped they put him in a dark cell and forgot about him.

"Are you ready?" Terran asked. "My friend has to get the digger back to the construction site by noon."

"Yes," I said, sidestepping the grassy plot. "Go ahead, dig him up."

The machine's engine roared to life. Birds from the neighboring tree evacuated, fluttering in mass toward the early morning sun.

I moved to the edge of the cemetery where Detective Richards stood with a steaming cup of coffee.

"What will you do with the remains?" he asked.

"Whatever is left of J.B. Towry will go to the crematorium. I'll make sure his ashes are poured into the local dump where they belong."

The detective sipped his coffee while Terran helped direct the machine's digger over the gate.

The grass was torn up from the machine leaving huge muddy tracks. If only there was some staff left to fix it after he left, but I had let everyone go fully paid for two weeks, perhaps longer if necessary. It had become evident White-hall Manor wasn't safe. If it took longer than two weeks, I'd pay for them to stay away the entire summer, but how much I depended on them had become evident in the last few days. The washing had begun to pile up along with the dishes and I couldn't expect Penelope to do everything.

A scraping noise sounded after a few minutes of digging. "Stop," I said, holding up a hand and rushing to the opening in the ground.

The rough sound of the digger ceased. Six feet down lay the top of the coffin, a wooden box with a cross carved into the top. Obviously, it hadn't helped convince J.B. Towry to go toward the light.

The detective finished his coffee and placed his cup at the edge of the cemetery and grabbed a nearby shovel.

With Terran's help, the two men dug along the edges of the coffin, removing the dirt and debris that kept them from opening the casket.

I watched from the end of the grave, staring down, ready to look into the empty sockets of J.B. Towry and damn him back to hell. This would be his last day at White-hall Manor. I shifted my gaze to the trees and listened for his protests. There were none. Not a whisper or threat in my ear. I scanned the front lawn and braced to feel his grip on my shoulders. Again, nothing.

Digging up his resting spot had to infuriate him and yet I sensed nothing.

With the area finally clear, the detective broke the coffin

lock using the edge of his shovel. It fell apart easily. A hundred-year-old lock along with some of the wood from the side of the coffin splintered easily.

"Ready?" Terran asked.

"Yes," I said, my heart thudding in my chest.

The detective and Terran shoved open the lid.

A heaviness sank into my stomach as I stared into the empty satin-lined coffin. My fingers fluttered to my throat. "W-where?"

"Nothing here," Terran said.

Detective Richard's eyes locked with mine.

I wanted to crawl down into the hole with them, to feel every inch of the lining for something to tell me what happened, but before I could lower myself down, Terran had his hand on my leg. "No way," he said. "Anne, it's over."

"But where? Where is he? Where's the body?"

The detective climbed out of the hole. He leaned the shovel against the fence. "I think you'll need to find the circumstances of his death to answer that question."

"He died in the institution in Baltimore," I said. "But he would have been buried here, wouldn't he? With the other Towrys. It was custom. Why would they bury an empty coffin or put a headstone if he wasn't buried here?"

Terran looked at me with concerned eyes and said, "You need to let this go. He's not here. He's not at Whitehall Manor."

The detective picked up his empty coffee cup. "I've got to get back to solving current crimes. Let me know if you discover anything."

"I will," I said as Terran closed the coffin and climbed out of the hole.

The backhoe roared to life again and gradually refilled the grave.

A few moments later the machine and its driver were gone. The detective, too. Terran had returned to the Marigold Garden to work on fertilizing the flowers. I wandered from the cemetery, searching my mind for how a haunting could occur without any remnants of the body. Had J.B. Towry the power to return to Whitehall Manor without his corpse?

His attachment to Whitehall Manor was far greater than I had realized, and J.B. Towry was far more powerful than I'd imagined. There must be a connection between him and the property that I could break, but how? I knew I had to tread carefully. I'd already asked too much of Terran.

Penelope met me at the doorstep with a steaming cup of decaffeinated coffee. "Any luck?" she asked.

I shook my head. "The coffin was empty." I took a sip of the warm drink as Penelope stared uncomfortably at me.

"It may not be the right time," she said, "but I'd like to talk to you about something you said at the party before all the chaos."

I remembered exactly my words to her. I had said I knew what was going on. I had all but stated outright that she was sleeping with my fiancé. "Maybe this isn't the right time."

"Yes, of course, but if there's anything I'm not doing correctly please—"

"No," I said, taking one more sip. "Let's talk later."

The truth was that I couldn't function without Penelope. If she left, things would fall apart. I had to be realistic. None of the staff were going to return to the house to work. No one was going to put in a job application any time soon. Penelope had to stay until things calmed down.

"Your grandfather arrived a few minutes ago," she said, taking the cup from me.

"Where?" I asked and she pointed to the orangery. Did I need to ask? Even with all the chaos over the last few days, Salazar showed up to tend to his trees.

I made my way around the drive to the building and went inside, finding him, snipping back dead leaves from a lemon tree.

"Salazar," I whispered.

He stopped his work. I needed his embrace and fell into his loving arms as he smoothed back my hair. Tears dripped to his coat. I pulled back and wiped my nose. "Seraphine would be so disappointed in me," I said.

It took him a moment, but he found a clean tissue from his pocket and gave it to me. I sat at the stone table and wiped the wetness from my cheeks.

"You shouldn't presume she'd think that," he said, sitting across from me.

"Look at what's happened." I turned toward the entertainment area where still, no matter how much he sprayed it with the hose, specks of blood from the boy and auctioneer's bodies could be seen.

"None of this is your fault. You did the best you could to put on a good party."

"I'm afraid," I said, plainly.

"The child who died. That was not your fault, and the party was very beautiful. You did your best. Is it the baby?"

My eyes met his and I sighed. "I've never felt this worried before." I never hid anything from Salazar, and I couldn't now. "There is a haunting here. I've known for months. I only wish I did something sooner."

"You said so at the party. I wasn't sure when you told me then, but now I think you're right."

"The ghost is J.B. Towry." I cringed at the next part but knew he had to have all the information. "He's my great-great-grandfather and he's also my great-great uncle."

Salazar's eyebrows kneaded together. "No."

"Something horrible happened here at Whitehall Manor over a hundred years ago. This man imprisoned his sister. He forced her to have children and he killed them. All except one who survived when Caroline escaped."

"She escaped and gave birth to—"

"My great grandfather. His name was Thomas Towry. He inherited Whitehall Manor after his mother's death. J.B. Towry was found too ill to stand trial and was sent to an asylum in Baltimore."

Salazar stood and took a breath.

I knew it was a lot. He had to be thinking about his daughter, my mother, Seraphine, and what he'd let her marry into. She had been only eighteen when she ran away with my father, a much older man. I remembered from the journals that they didn't approve. Salazar had said it was rumors that made him hesitant. Now, he was seeing those rumors had truth to them.

"What should I do?" I said, a tone of desperation in my voice. "I think the ghost possessed that boy and made him kill himself."

"You must get him to leave."

"But how?"

Salazar returned to the table. His eyes searched mine. "You are sure the ghost is here?"

"Yes. I thought digging up his bones would help. I thought ridding his remains from Whitehall Manor would break his attachment to the land, but his body is not buried in the Towry Cemetery. It must have been buried in Baltimore when he died."

"Then you must go to Baltimore. You must make sure that his soul is at rest."

"Soul? What soul?" I stared dejected at the floor. "The ghost is evil. There's no reasoning with it."

He sat down and shifted in his chair. "You must not give up."

"I have a baby coming at the end of the summer. I don't know if it's worth it to stay here. Maybe we should close up the manor and move into town."

"No, then he wins. He gets what he wants." He stared firmly into my eyes. "Your mother did not give up her life so that you would walk away easily from challenges. She wanted you here. She worked to change the future of this home for you. You must not give up finishing what she started."

I knew Salazar was right. I couldn't let J.B. Towry take over Whitehall Manor. I had to make sure he had no claim and that his power didn't grow.

"You must go to Baltimore," Salazar said. "You must go find where his body is and make sure the attachment he has to Whitehall Manor is severed forever."

I gnawed at my finger, and he snapped for me to stop. "Do not give up on your claim to this land. Remember your mother is buried here. She watches out for you. Your strength is in the land. If you leave for good, then you will have nothing."

I knew my grandfather was right. This was my home. I had to stay, and I wasn't willing to share it with J.B. Towry.

CHAPTER

SEVENTEEN

I t had been over six months since I last drove to Baltimore. I took a moment to gaze across the city from the hill where I sat. An early morning hue of late May sun illuminated the buildings turning them black against a golden sky. Natural energy pulsed in the city as cars worked their way through back alleys and factories puffed out white smoke that clashed against seagulls cawing in the sky.

I ate the last of my breakfast sandwich and tossed the wrapper into a nearby can. What I had missed the most about the city was freedom. I had lived for years in blissful ignorance, unaware of the happenings of Whitehall Manor but now I knew too much. I could never go back. Returning to Whitehall gave me so much but each step of my progress came with pitfalls and tragedy.

What I knew to be true in my heart was that I needed Whitehall Manor as much as it needed me. I needed a place to belong, a home to raise my child, a love that was mine and mine alone, and most importantly a connection to my past. Without it, as Salazar had said, I would be lost forever.

And Whitehall Manor needed my strength to direct its energy. It would take it from whoever claimed rights to the land, but the property could not serve two masters. The ghost of J.B. Towry had to go.

As I headed back to my car, I knew I'd have to drive across the city to what had been known as the Baltimore Asylum for the Criminally Insane to meet with the records keeper. I had twenty minutes until then, so I took one last look out across the city. I recalled enjoying my small apartment near the waterfront back when I had been alone and struggling. I shrugged away those thoughts. There was the past and then there was the distant past. I had to stay focused on pulling the threads through to smooth out the timeline, to make my existence in the present, and the future of our child safe.

Twenty minutes later, I pulled into the parking lot of the institution, which was now a more modernized facility than I imagined it was back in the eighteen hundreds when J.B. Towry was brought here. A few rats lingered near an overflowing trash can and the hint of something rotten lingered in the musty air. I hurried across the cracked asphalt toward the front door.

Several people sat out front. Two people in wheelchairs sat alone on the front walk and I wondered if someone even knew they were there. A woman hunched over on the curb smoked a cigarette and picked something from her arm that wasn't there. A man dug through a plastic bag and pulled out a half-eaten sandwich.

"They have to buzz you in," said a security guard leaning against the hospital's entrance. "Do they know you're coming?"

"Yes," I muttered. "I have an appointment."

"We have appointments, too," someone said.

127

So, this was a line of patients waiting to be seen. Perhaps without appointments. I pressed the call button. It crackled to life. A voice on the other end said, "Hello?" in a sharp tone.

"My name is Anne Towry. I'm here to speak to the records keeper. I have an appointment."

The door buzzed and I quickly opened it. The minute I walked through the first door, an overwhelming scent of urine hit my senses and made me gag. I covered my nose with my sleeve and pressed the second button to be let in. It, too, clicked open, and I hurried inside.

The Baltimore Asylum for the Criminally Insane was now a state-run hospital renamed Baltimore's Health Center with limited resources and even more limitations to their building and décor. As I worked my way toward the front desk, I passed dozens of chairs with people sleeping. Someone coughed and it sounded as if they were on their last breath.

"Can I help you?" a woman asked at the front desk.

"I have a meeting today. I'm Anne Towry." I showed her my identification.

She turned toward her computer.

My eyes scanned more of the room. At least thirty people were crowded into chairs. I sighed as it became clear that having an appointment didn't mean much and I'd more than likely be here all day. I glanced at the time. Terran would wonder where I was. I would have to make up an excuse. I couldn't let him know I was still on the hunt for more clues to the haunting. Our relationship was already on thin ice by my dogged persistence.

"Take a seat," the woman said, handing back my ID. "I'll call you when she gets here."

My shoulders slumped and I half thought of leaving but

couldn't. I needed to know what happened to J.B. Towry. I needed to find out where he was buried. I slunk to the first open seat that didn't have something glued to it.

Hours passed. Only a few more patients were buzzed in. I couldn't imagine the number of people who needed help and waited all day, but then there were the priority patients, the ones who were buzzed in immediately, and escorted by police officers. These patients were screaming, twisting, and moaning in the officers' hands.

I ran my fingers through my hair. How could they tolerate their cries day in and day out? People at the edge of their sanity. Others who had clearly plunged off the deep end into something they may never recover from. The whole room pulsed with tension and sadness. How I wished I could return to Whitehall Manor and the dealings of one lunatic ghost. As long as I had the gardens, the fresh air, and the loving embrace of Terran, I could manage anything, even the constant threat of a haunting. I clutched my bag and stood to leave when suddenly I felt a flutter in my belly.

I lowered back to the chair and pressed my fingers to my stomach. It was the first time I had felt the baby move. My child had kicked or shifted inside of me. Tears welled in my eyes. Everything became real to me at that moment. I would be a mother in three months and J.B. Towry would be after my child, determined to destroy any threat to his claim. I couldn't leave now. I couldn't ignore the problem, and I was the only person who could put an end to it.

"Ms. Towry?" a pleasant voice called out.

My gaze shifted to the woman standing next to the front desk. She held her folded hands in front of her. Her dark hair matched her equally dark eyes. A pleasant smile widened her mouth and I slowly stood and went to her.

"I'm Chantelle Grace," she said, shaking my hand. "I understand you need information about a loved one."

"Yes, I mean he was a distant relative of mine. I'd like to see his records if they still exist."

"Follow me," she said. She led me through a door and past a series of offices into a back room where it was much quieter and smelled of stale coffee and fresh donuts. The lighting was good here, too, a soft glow that made my breathing even out. I scanned the other people in their offices on phones and meeting with patients at their desks.

Once we were in her office, I sat in a chair across from her. "I appreciate you meeting me on such short notice."

She smiled revealing a nice set of white teeth as she sat. "It was harder to find this file than I thought it would be. We have had several fires and floods over the last hundred or so years. Some of them were intentional, unfortunately. Others were accidental. We've lost so many records to that and time."

"I had no idea there had been a fire," I said.

"We've housed our fair share of arsonists. But some of the fires were due to simply poor installation. The facility was created not long after the Civil War ended, and your relative's record was part of the oldest files we have for the facility. I found it locked up in one of the cabinets down in the basement."

"There's a basement?"

"Oh, yes. We use it for storage now but back in the eighteen hundreds it is where your great-great-grandfather would have been held. We've come a long way in mental health care since then but at that time they would have put someone like J.B. Towry in a cell with minimal assistance."

It was as I'd imagined. Thrown in a dark cell, fending off

rats at night and screams of fellow patients during the day. It is exactly what he deserved.

Ms. Grace opened the file in front of her.

I could see the edges were worn. There was water damage to the front of the paper.

"Your great-great-grandfather was an interesting man."

"You've read the file?"

"Most of it."

"And you're not shocked?"

She shook her head. "His crimes are horrific, but his mental state would have been at the level of total incapacitation. He would have fluctuated between reality and fantasy on a daily basis. His deep-seated rage would have manifested in ways that most of us would have been horrified to witness. Unfortunately, the methods of treatment in the eighteen hundreds were nothing short of barbaric. Many doctors thought patients were controlled by demons. Can you imagine?"

"It seems like something possesses them, doesn't it?"

"It's all part of psychiatric pathology. We would have treated your relative with medication and therapy today."

"And that ... works for everyone?"

"No, not everyone. Some people must stay institutionalized for the safety of our community."

I examined the woman wondering how she could be so calm. She had read his file. She must have known medication and therapy would never have worked for J.B. Towry. He was a sadist. She knew he had killed nine newborn children, and raped and imprisoned his sister.

She shuffled through the papers in the file.

The old worn folder was more of a collection of papers than an actual proper record.

"You said he fluctuated between reality and fantasy."

"Yes," she said. "They didn't have a word for it until closer to when he died, but he was more than likely a paranoid schizophrenic with elements of psychosis."

"What could have caused this?"

"We still don't know for sure. Genetics, environmental conditions, quality of food, the conditions in utero." Her gaze shifted to my growing belly.

I placed a hand there. "I know this will sound strange, but do you believe in hauntings?"

She pressed her lips together and leaned forward. "Do you believe in hauntings?"

I felt if I asked her another question, it would be one question too many. If I pushed it, she might offer me a hospital stay free of charge and a thorough mental exam. Instead, I laughed and shifted in my chair. "No," I said. "I wondered because the building is so old."

"It is," she said. "Housed many soldiers who couldn't come to grips with reality after the war." She stood and pushed the file toward me. "I'll give you some time alone. Let me know if you have any questions."

"I will," I said as I slipped off my jacket.

Slowly opening the file, I saw the handwriting of the physician who cared for him. It was practically illegible. I flipped through a few more pages. There were more notes updating J.B. Towry's condition. The dates were clear. He had been admitted to the institution in the fall of 1881 at the age of forty-three. The notes said he was admitted after a brief hospital stay in which he was recovering from miasma or bad air which afterward was scratched out and the word malaria written over it. He was transferred to the sanatorium upon recovery with what the doctors wrote was an unclear madness that drove him to speak to beings that didn't exist and a desire to torture those who did.

I shuddered at those words thinking of Caroline and how she had suffered because of his deteriorating mind. I flipped through to a few photographs. These were the first ones I had seen that were actual photos from the early nineteen hundreds. His thick bushy hair seen in the earlier daguerreotype was gone. In these pictures his face was gaunt. The dark circles around his eyes showed his lack of sleep or perhaps his tortured mind. There wasn't a hair on his head. He looked nothing like the ghost that sat watching me in my sleep and joined me in my nightmares but still had the familiar haunting glare of an evil mindset. He reminded me of a war victim and in a way whatever tormented him must have made it feel as if a battle raged in his head.

The later notes showed signs of developing conditions and deeper understanding of his condition. The first time the word schizophrenia was used was in 1918, only three years before his death. I scanned the notes to see the words that reminded me of Father. "Obsessively cruel to the other patients, attacking several, killing one, found eating his remains before staff could tranquilize him."

Page after page of details showed J.B. Towry's abject cruelty toward others. His mind wavered as Ms. Grace said between psychosis and reality, between terror and depression, and with no other useful remedies than the long list of tried and failed treatments they used starting on the first day of his admittance to the asylum. I scanned the words:

Purges
Emetics
Bloodletting
Blows
Restraints

Straight jacket
Simulated drowning
Starvation
Swinging chair

I SHIVERED. He had tortured others and in return, they had tortured him, but none of the treatments changed J.B. Towry. The following pages included his notes, an unrelenting sick fantasy of events at Whitehall Manor, that he relived through storytelling and graphic and obscene drawings.

In this part, the doctor's notes were clear.

"The following letters were taken from J.B. Towry upon discovery of his collection of writings kept inside the stone wall of his cell. It is unclear how he got access to paper and pen to write these notes. The letters reveal his true state of psychosis."

I shifted in my chair. I came to find out where his body was buried but instead, I was looking into J.B. Towry's head. I had done that once before when reading his journal. It had not helped me but instead sent me spiraling into mania and chaos. Did I dare read his thoughts again? I looked around the room. Where better to take this risk than a lunatic asylum? If I did step off the deep end, Ms. Grace would have me hauled to treatment.

Again, it came to me that the more information I knew the better my chances of defeating him, ending his reign of terror at Whitehall Manor for good. I took a deep breath and began to read.

EIGHTEEN

J ohn Burton Towry
      Case # 39209
      Diagnosis: Dementia
    Age: 47
Imprisonment: Life
Prognosis: Terminal disease of the mind

I KNOW NOT what day nor what hour it is. Years have blended in this pit of a prison. Fear not for my comfort. I have the memories of the past to keep me company. I have the bloody scent of my sister's dead children on my hands to bring me peace.

In my time, I've been able to relive my sister's death over and over again to such joy and delight I cannot describe. I envision them laying your body beneath the ground. I saw your weakened and skeletal form finally give in after they carved out your son from your belly. If I could, I would kill your son like I killed the others. I would tear his limbs apart and scatter them to the four corners of the property. I'd feed his torso to my hawks. I'd bury his head upside down in the fields.

Alas, envisioning your burial brought no relief. I had spent years torturing you and now I only tortured myself with wishes and desires.

No longer do I dread the bloodletting rituals of these sadist doctors. They hoist me up by rope and tear into my flesh with their knives each day from the moment I wake until I fall into a deep trembling stupor.

"Keep him calm," they say. "Keep him sedated."

When the bloodletting fails, I am more aggravated than before. I was blamed for the attack on my cellmate. I tore apart his face and devoured his heart. But it is they who are to blame for awakening the darkest parts of my soul, driving me further into my madness through their torture, and starving me of my sanity. How else could I find nourishment? The man's heart gave me strength. Drinking his blood gave me clarity.

They would keep me chained all day to the wall, naked and covered in my own excrement, if they could. Nothing would bring them more satisfaction than to keep me locked in this dark cell for life. If only they could throw away the key. Some doctors have cursed me. I laughed at them and spit in their faces. Some have been driven near mad themselves. I've witnessed one particularly weak-spirited physician take the blade he used to drain me of my blood and run it across his own wrists.

They blamed me for that incident. But again, it is their fault. They brought this on themselves by torturing my soul from its body. The endless purges they subject me to are means for me to leave myself entirely. As my physical form lays unmoving on the floor, a pool of vomit surrounding me, my soul bears witness from the corner of the cell.

The physicians laugh. They've finally subdued me or so they think.

"He'll be quiet now," one doctor says.

"A little more should keep him down for the rest of the week," another one says.

Their barbaric practices only strengthened my ability to leave my body and enter the physical form of others. When I left my body the first time, I became curious and lingered by my cot awaiting the demons of hell. I had been told time and time again that when I died, I would be greeted by them and dragged to the hell from whence I came. I clutched the frame of my bed and searched the darkened room for their wicked faces.

When no one came, I laughed.

I looked forward to the next treatment. The doctors brought me to awareness then turned around and cut open my veins, draining me of blood to the point that I once again slipped from my body. In the minutes that followed, I had free reign over the asylum and ran from cell to cell rattling the cages of my enemies, tossing their food bowls into the air and digging my nails into their flesh.

It then came to me that I was capable of so much more. I turned toward the doctor. I had been tortured long enough. I fixed my gaze on him and wormed my way inch by inch into his body, forcing out his own soul until I had full possession of the man. It was then I dragged the blade across his wrists and watched in delight as the second doctor screamed for me to stop.

No sooner had they dragged his near-dead body from my jail cell, did I slip back into my own body, returning to full awareness of my power. For years following this incident, I craved their torture, begging for more until the treatments stopped. For years there was nothing and I was forced to blood-let myself. Then, they put me in a room where I could do nothing to harm myself but I found ways to deprive myself of oxygen until I woke to the straitjacket and inability to move for days on end. Alas, I agreed to comply with the new treatments as their methods were ever-evolving.

But the doctors changed over the years. Young doctors never stay. Old doctors die. They bring in so-called experts from Germany to watch me as if I'm an ape in a cage. They tied my hands and dragged me from the cell to their torture chambers, secured in a straitjacket, plunging me into buckets of ice-cold water in the hopes that it would shock me back to reality.

In one experiment, they succeeded in killing me. I took the water into my lungs and a darkness descended in front of me unlike anything I had previously seen. I had been plunged into hell. A hell of blackness. Of nothingness. It was not the hell I had expected. There were no demons. Satan did not sit on his throne awaiting my presence.

No, instead of a fiery pit of hell, I awoke to the shimmering waters of Willow Creek. I was whole in my flesh beneath a blue sky and full sun. I turned to gaze at Whitehall Manor, its pure white majesty glistened in the heat. It was the only sense of peace I'd had in years. I would return to my home to die. I saw how I would be buried there. I saw who stood beside me at the final moment of my death. I realized I was the one true owner and would be sure that it never passed into another's hands.

As hollow voices in the distance yelled out, "You've killed him, doctor. You've killed him" I made my way toward the Towry cemetery, toward the graves of my ancestors. Beneath the willow tree, I scanned their headstones. Generations of powerful men lay before me. None of them could do what I could. None could return to life after death. I felt the pull of my spirit toward the darkened hole of the asylum. I would not go yet. Not without leaving a reminder that I was here.

My gaze fell on my dear sister's grave. The angel's protective arms surrounded her and infuriated me. I marched to it and knocked the head from the statue, watching it tumble to the ground and laughing. I could move between realities. It was the most profound realization.

The men pulled me from the water and pounded on my chest and again I was in the hellhole of the asylum, gasping for air.

"Take him back to his cell," the doctor ordered.

In a weakened state, I was hauled through the grimy corridors, past the rats, and lunatics clinging from their cages. I was tossed to my cot and lay there for hours piecing together the experience of leaving my body.

I had found a way to get my revenge. The path was cleared for me. From that day forward, I held to one belief. I would survive the years in the asylum and find my way back to Whitehall Manor. I would die there as I had seen in my vision but I would never leave. I would survive the years of torture that lay before me until I made my return and secured my proper place at my childhood home as owner and master of the land and Towry fortune no matter how long it took.

-J.B. Towry

CHAPTER

NINETEEN

I took a deep breath. His words coursed through my veins. J.B. Towry was anything but insane. The torturous methods they used on him only clarified his purpose. What I knew at that moment was that J.B. Towry was pure evil. His determination matched the worst of criminals who knew that patience could bring them to their ultimate goal. I shuddered as I closed the file when suddenly a piece of paper floated to the ground.

Staring at it, I saw that it was written on the same old paper as the previous one, in the same handwriting and signed by J.B. Towry. I dared not guess what other psychotic foretellings it contained. I leaned over and picked it up, smoothing it out on the desk before me feeling a tremor works its way into my hand.

DEAREST ANNE,

Rest assured that I watch over you. You and your unborn child will meet the same fate as my dear sister, Caroline. I bide my time as I linger in your dreams, studying you and knowing your strengths and weaknesses. Dare not continue your investigation into my bond with Whitehall Manor. It is for me and only me to know. I am the dark heart that beats in the belly of the beast. Your curiosity will eventually be your undoing.

I relish the day that I get my hands on your precious baby. I know already that it will be a boy and you will name him Christopher. You will try to take me from what is destined to be mine. You will fail. I will take your child first and drown him in the creek. Once his bloated, blue body floats helplessly away with the tide, I will return for you. Your screams of pain and torture will delight me. I will keep you locked in the cage I'm making for you right now. I will torture you day and night. You will fulfill all of my wicked desires.

For the rest of your miserable life, I will ensure your suffering. Your loved ones will all run screaming from Whitehall Manor. Your servants will leave or be murdered in ways that serve my delight. One by one those who remain to help you will meet an ungodly end.

You've been warned to leave Whitehall Manor. If you choose to stay, you choose your death and the wretched deaths of everyone who comes near you.

-J.B. Towry

I sat back in my chair and trembled. I felt sickened to my core. How? How was this possible? How was I reading a letter from someone who had died a hundred years ago? It was impossible, but no. I chewed my lip, touching it and feeling blood then quickly dug through my purse for a tissue that I pressed to the spot.

I knew J.B. Towry was a ghost. He had awareness even then that foretold the future. My eyes scanned the words of the letter again. My heart thudded in my chest. Another passage seemed to be written before me as my eyes watched. No, it wasn't a passage. It was a drawing. As the outline came to form, I recognized it. It was me, naked, in my bed at Whitehall Manor. My god, it made no sense. A cold shock worked its way down my spine.

Then, another letter. I read the words as they formed until finally the whole paragraph was complete. Sickened, I dropped the file and yelled for Ms. Grace to return.

It took a moment but the tapping of her shoes down the hallway neared. She came into the room. "Is everything okay?" she asked, breathless.

"No, is this some kind of joke?"

"What is it?"

I picked up the file and handed it to her. "The last letter in the file."

She hurried to sit down at her desk, put on her glasses, and flipped through the pages. "This one?"

"Yes."

Her eyes widened as she read the words. "I don't know how to explain this," she said.

"That last letter details J.B. Towry's actions at my house, at Whitehall Manor, only days ago. A ten-year-old boy killed a man at my house then himself. A woman died, too, accidentally in the chaos. This happened only days ago. How is this letter in the file?"

"It's unexplainable," she said.

I took the file from her and read his words. *"He is ten years old. He picks up my journal. He's a fool. A blind, curious fool. But that's not why I will kill him. I will kill him to ruin her party. I've given her the choice. She's chosen war. Anne Towry must leave or I will kill everything and everyone she loves until she does."* I lowered the page. "Are you telling me you didn't write this?"

"No, Ms. Towry. I did not write this letter."

"Someone else in your office then?"

"I brought the file up from the basement before I met with you. Before that, it had been in a locked filing cabinet for over a hundred years."

My stomach churned. The breakfast sandwich I ate earlier threatened to come up. "There's only one explanation then," I said. "Your treatments worked."

"*Our* treatments?"

"Bloodletting, purging him of his stomach contents, dunking him in ice-cold baths. Should I go on?"

"I've told you, Ms. Towry, those are barbaric methods of the eighteen hundreds. We can't be held responsible for what they believed would have worked back then."

I swallowed. "But don't you see, they did work. Read his letter. They gave him insight into his condition as they had hoped. Only, the truth of the matter is that J.B. Towry grew stronger with these realizations. He figured out how to overcome death. How to get what he wanted not for the moment or even a lifetime. He learned how to get what he wanted for eternity."

Ms. Grace sat back in her chair. She was quiet for a moment and then said, "Ms. Towry, is there someone I can call for you? Someone to come get you?"

"No," I said. "I'm better, too. This information has helped me better understand who or what I'm dealing with. There's one more thing I need to know."

The woman looked clearly uncomfortable. Her hands slipped below the desk and I wondered if she had a panic button of some sort beneath it.

"Please, Ms. Grace. I understand what I'm saying is bizarre, but unless you can explain the letters in his file, you'll have to believe me."

She paused and then took a breath. "I have someone else coming in. I think it would be best if you leave."

"I will. Tell me what happened to J.B. Towry's body. Where was he buried? Where are the notes about his death?"

It was clear she wanted me to leave but I wasn't going anywhere until I knew.

She picked up the file and flipped through it. "The record indicates he was released."

"Released?" I said. "To whom? When?"

"There was a horrible fire in 1921. It burned the asylum nearly to the ground. Your relative would have been moved from the institution to a shelter at that time."

"J.B. Towry died in 1921," I said.

She scanned through some of the illegible writing that I had not been able to make out. "Some of the patients were released to their families. It looks like the doctor believed that John Burton Towry was no longer a threat. He would have been in his eighties by that time, hardly a worry to the community at that age, so he may have been released."

I cringed, knowing the terror he was still capable of no matter what his age. "Where did he go?"

"It's hard to say, but it looks..." She examined the notes more closely. "Oh, yes." She flipped the page over and scanned it. "Here it is. He was released on September 23, 1921, to Thomas Towry. The final address is listed as White-hall Manor."

I closed my eyes. He had fulfilled his wish. He waited them out and won. He had found a way to return.

"Do you know that name?" she asked.

My eyes flashed open. "Yes, he was my great-grandfather. Why would he have agreed to take the man who killed his mother?"

"That I can't answer for you." She handed the folder to me. "You can take this file. Maybe it will help you figure out whatever it is you're trying to figure out."

I shoved the file into my bag and stood to leave. "Thank you for your help."

She stared at me for a moment and then said, "You know, Ms. Towry, there is such a thing as forgiveness. Perhaps your great-grandfather found it when he decided to take home J.B. Towry."

I pressed my lips together knowing that what Thomas Towry brought home was a shell of a human that forgiveness could never reach.

CHAPTER

TWENTY

B ack at my car, there was a ticket on the windshield and a dent in the fender. It didn't matter. I got what I needed. A little damage to my car was a price worth paying to find out that J.B. Towry had been released to his son, Thomas Towry, which meant he had been brought back to Whitehall Manor, but why?

I got into the car and started the ignition. The afternoon sun had shifted the light on the buildings. An eerie sensation coursed through me as I sat thinking about what I had learned. Returning to Whitehall Manor could mean the end of everyone I love. I held a hand to my growing baby bump.

What J.B. Towry was capable of was far beyond what I could manage. He could slip in and out of my dreams, possess any one of us at any moment, or insight us to murder if he desired. I tried to think of why he hadn't. Why was he waiting to do any of those things? The answer came to me quickly. After reading his letters it was clear he enjoyed the torture.

He was slowly driving us all insane, driving us apart, taking lives when he wanted, and all of it was to entertain him, but I knew what he ultimately wanted. He wanted control, and so did I. The only difference was that I could physically take it while he only could try to.

I drove out of the parking lot and toward the interstate. I would not let him keep me from what was mine. I'd return home to Whitehall Manor and force him out. Only I had to figure out the last few pieces of the puzzle.

Why would Thomas not have let his father rot in some other asylum? I remembered the information the archivist gave me. Thomas had been known for reprising Whitehall Manor. He had taken over when he turned eighteen, married not long after that, and had a son. The article said he had doubled the Towry fortune through good investments. It didn't make sense. Why would he risk everything to bring a criminal back to the manor?

As I merged onto the interstate it dawned on me that perhaps he didn't bring him back. Perhaps Thomas removed him from the shelter following the fire but then drove him to the woods and left him there or forced him off a cliff or shoved him in the root cellar to die his last days in darkness. I imagined the joy and relief he would have felt to know he got revenge on J.B. Towry. If that was the case, though, how on earth would I ever find his remains?

Detective Richards had been all over the property when searching for Maura Wells. He and his team searched every inch of ground for large bodies as he said. J.B. Towry was a large body. He would have found him for sure if he was buried on the grounds.

The question about the empty coffin still lingered, too. Why would Thomas have put an empty coffin into the ground, a fake headstone, and then only two years later killed himself? I needed more answers but everyone who could give me answers was dead. The archivist had nothing more. Where could I go to find the truth?

My phone rang. Terran's name flashed on the car monitor. I chewed nervously on my thumbnail. Should I answer it? He would know I was in the car, but I could say I was coming back from town. A horrible lie to the man I loved. I tapped the steering wheel and then decided to ignore the call. I didn't need another fight. If he asked when I got back, then I would say something, but I hoped he didn't.

A part of me felt that Terran must already know that I'd never give up trying to find the truth. Perhaps he had accepted that this was the new normal for our relationship. Don't ask, don't tell. Oh, but that was horrible, too.

How could we move forward in our relationship if we knew the space between us was widening? But if I told him the truth then he might leave. I flicked on the radio to distract myself. There was over an hour left on my drive and I couldn't keep worrying about things I couldn't control.

Once over the bridge, the traffic began to thin. I desperately wanted to stop after passing my third sign for fried chicken, but I didn't. I had to get back to Whitehall Manor. The day was nearly ending, and I had to be there.

As I turned onto the road to Ashbury, a sudden chill went through me. It was as if the closer I got to Whitehall Manor the more the sensation worked its way into my core. I flicked on the car's heater, cranking it as high as it would go. It was a poor substitute for the warmth of the fire in the sitting room but worked to push the achy cold from my body.

The phone rang again. This time it was Penelope. I wondered if she needed direction on what to do with all the gear left behind by the caterers. It would have to be brought back to them at some point since none of them would return to the manor.

I clicked accept. "Hello, Penelope."

Her voice was garbled. There was static as I tried to make out what she was saying. I was nearly back now, only a few more minutes. Damn these communication lines. When would the county catch up with the rest of the world?

"I can't hear you," I said to her. "But I'll be back in a few minutes. Is this about dinner?"

Again, more garbled noise. As I reached to end the call, I heard the dreaded words, "Salazar ... is ... dead."

PART THREE
JULY

TWENTY-ONE

I t took a few minutes but finally, I had the fire going again, roaring to life. The warmth quickly filled the room and felt like a protection around me that I needed. The fire would remain burning, I vowed. Despite the hot sticky weather of July that made the heat pulse from the driveway and sweat trickle down my back, I would not extinguish the heart of Whitehall Manor. Not when I knew J.B. Towry had succeeded in fulfilling his promise written in that note. He had killed the person I loved most dearly and would come for all of us, one by one.

In the days that followed Salazar's death, a black cloud loomed over Whitehall Manor. A storm blew up the bay unleashing a torrent of rain that overfilled the pool and sent waves crashing against the shoreline.

Penelope worked tirelessly to keep up with the work of managing the home, lighting candles in every room when the power went out, and rushing to maintain her high standards of cleanliness, but eventually, it was agreed that it was too much. We shut the doors to the rooms no longer in use, locking each one, drawing us closer together.

"You should leave," I said to her finally. "All the staff is gone now."

"I won't leave you, Anne," she said.

It touched my heart, but I couldn't help but wonder if it was me she wouldn't leave or Terran. I desperately wanted to warn her of the danger and finally against my better judgment said, "There's a curse here. I am cursed. If you don't leave, you may suffer."

She stared at me with kind eyes, those kind eyes that made me feel like a subject of her pity, an awful, twisted wreck. "I can handle it," she said.

In the evenings, sitting by the fire, as the storm progressed and lashed against the side of the house, I'd stare at Terran and him at me. We'd transfer our thoughts through long stares of love and worry. Salazar had been the only person who believed me. He'd never doubted my concerns when I brought them to him. He always listened with an open heart. I should have known he'd be the first of my loved ones J.B. Towry would target.

As I turned my gaze toward the fire, I remembered the day I returned home from Baltimore, rushing into the house, tears staining my cheeks, searching for Terran and proof that my grandfather was dead.

I found them in the orangery.

On the floor, Salazar's body had been laid out not far from where the other deaths had occurred.

"What happened?" I cried, falling to my knees beside his body.

Terran eased away from Penelope. I didn't miss anything, least of all how they stood only inches apart as if they'd been embracing.

"Anne," Terran said. "He's gone. It was a heart attack. He went quickly."

"No," I moaned. "I can't lose him, too. I can't."

Terran pulled me into his arms. The soft scent of his skin pressed onto my cheek. "Let me take you inside," he whispered.

"I want to be left alone with him."

"I'll call for the coroner," Penelope said, easing her way past us.

"It's not good for you," he said. "He's gone. There's nothing that could have been done."

I wanted to stay with Salazar to at least reassure him that his death would not be in vain, but there was no use. I couldn't make promises anymore. I was wrecked.

A crack overhead and a loud thud outside the window pulled me back. I was now alone by the fire. The storm still raged. I turned to see Terran standing at the edge of the room. He had been watching me. Had I been talking to myself? I touched my raw lips.

He raised his dark brows, and I knew what he was thinking. This is where Father sat and then Lucinda Warner after him, always by the fire, always trying to protect themselves from something and now I was doing the same.

"Please, come to bed," he said. "I'll keep you warm."

"No," I said. "Stay here. The fire will keep us safe."

"From the storm?" he asked and then he shook his head. He knew what I meant. He turned and disappeared.

I wanted to go after him, but it was too late. I had to protect the baby. The voices grew stronger at night, and I couldn't leave the fire. As the storm went on, the sound of dripping came from somewhere nearby. I strained my neck to see it was the bayside window. The sound pulsed throughout the night as I fought against sleep.

But exhaustion wore me down and soon I was drifting into a heaviness that wasn't my own. Salazar stood in the orangery. He reached for a pomegranate. It fell and rolled into the darkened grotto. I began to pant, sharp breaths in and out as sweat trickled down my cheek. "Don't go," I said. "Don't go in there."

Salazar was oblivious to my cries and rightly so. The events of my dream had passed. I was an observer of what had already occurred. I twisted in my sleep. Salazar went to retrieve the fruit when suddenly the demented face of J.B. Towry appeared from the darkness. The air thickened with the scent of tobacco and death. "No!" I cried out. Salazar clutched his throat as he tried to take a breath and fight back against the entity that tormented him.

A dark well of emptiness appeared into which Salazar was pulled. Clutching his chest, he fell back to a chair, open-mouthed, eyes fixed into a state of pure horror.

I was startled awake. In the night, I had twisted my neck into a wretched state. I massaged it. The storm had finally broken. Outside, the sun pushed through the clouds.

The morning hours were my favorite, especially following a storm. I opened the door. The scents of rich soil mingled with water and blossoms of opening flowers. They released soft perfumed smells around me. I stepped onto the wet grass. Puddles had formed all over the garden. The pool was flooded with the corpses of dead frogs and rodents who hadn't survived the night.

A paper floated in the water that I fished out and read. Disbelieving it at first, I stared in horror at a page from J.B. Towry's journal. It had survived the fire and floated up through the chimney. To where it went next, I didn't know, only that it had blown back in the storm and landed before me with the words, "*You're next*" written clearly before me.

I fell to the ground and dug my hands into the earth. What would befall me and my child? I tried to force back the pictures but they came anyway. I saw myself kept prisoner by a ghost in the house, tormented and starved as Caroline had been.

I took handfuls of earth and shoved the black dirt into my pockets. Then I scooped up more and shoved it into my mouth, chewing slowly, staring vacantly out to the water, while my mind filtered out all the horrible experiences of trying to force Whitehall to be something it wasn't. So many people had died here. The guilt pressed into me.

It was my fault that I had been so brazen to think I could turn the manor home into anything other than the haunted house that it was.

I took another handful of dirt and ate from it tasting the dark soil and nutrients as they slid down my throat. I knew I had to read more of J.B. Towry's journal, but it was impossible. We had burned it. Perhaps there was something else. Something in the attic I hadn't found before. I turned to look back at the manor and saw in the upstairs window where my mother had fought for her life, a looming figure, a shadow looking down, watching me still, and heard his whispering voice in my head. My god, Terran was in that room.

I pulled myself up and hurried to the bedroom to find no one there, only the lingering scent of smoke. Terran's side of the bed had not been slept in. When I scanned the closet, I knew the reason why. He had left me. I collapsed into tears. It was better that he left than suffer the same as Salazar, but it was my worst fear coming true. I was nearly alone again.

I had one person left in the world and that person wasn't even born yet. I held my swollen belly, nearly eight months now. The baby would be here soon, and I was no closer to solving this mystery than when I left Baltimore two months ago. My time was running out. I wandered to the baby's room and pushed open the door to see the room had been transformed.

My hand pressed to my chest as I took in the mural along the wall. Where there had been neutral paint to replace the yellow wallpaper, there was now a clean coat of soft blue pastel. Why had I not come to this room in the last two months? I knew the answer. I knew this had been J.B. Towry's childhood room. This had been where he first formed his wicked mind and evil ways, but it was no longer that.

In all my determination to find answers, I had not noticed the work being done around me. I stepped to the mural and searched for the signature. It was there in the bottom right-hand corner.

Salazar

How he had found time following the charity event and his passing to paint this, I didn't know. I laughed and felt my heart soar. It was the first time I'd felt well in weeks. He had painted a perfect mural of the shoreline along the wall. An image of seagulls and blue herons. A friendly crab with a raised claw as if it were waving. The rippling waters of Willow Creek were perfectly captured. In the distance, a sailboat. The water was peppered with remote islands and children playing along the sand. I couldn't help but notice a beautiful woman with long flowing dark hair standing near the shoreline, surrounded by marigolds. My mother, Seraphine.

A tear dripped down my cheek. It was an act of genuine kindness that I wasn't used to. A message from beyond of Salazar's strength and determination to help me on my quest. The rest of the room had been set up. The crib was put together with a dangling mobile of marigolds. Beside it was a changing table. As I stepped to the cabinet, I caught a glimpse inside the closet. It was filled with baby clothes. All sizes from newborn to one year.

I stifled a smile. For the first time in a long while, I felt excited for the baby's arrival. Instead of the fear that pulsed through me nearly every waking moment, I felt joy. I sat in the rocking chair, gazing around the room.

There was time left, six weeks, and I had to pull myself together to end this. I rose from the chair as a hawk landed outside the window. I narrowed my eyes at it, and I knew I'd have to go back in the attic to search for more clues to answer the question of why Thomas Towry brought J.B. Towry back to Whitehall Manor and what drove him to kill himself.

TWENTY-TWO

M y dried blood was still on the floor. I ignored it and searched the wardrobe for any other letters or journals that would give me the answers I sought. Despite the insulation in the attic, it was still stiflingly hot. As each minute passed and the sun grew stronger, the heat increased.

I wouldn't let that stop me. I tore apart the drawers and dumped their contents onto the floor. When I couldn't find anything, I moved to another part of the attic and began searching there.

An old trunk had more things that would have been great to auction at the charity event. Too late now. I found more books and flipped through them to see they were nothing but history and cartography information. At the bottom of the trunk, there was something else. I pulled out several postcards. A string surrounded them. I quickly untied it and scanned the photographs. One of Paris. Another of London. A third of Rome. I flipped them over. They were from Thomas's wife but were written to him. But he had gone with her, hadn't he?

No, I read through the messages. She had arrived in Paris with their son. Much of it was a retelling of her travels and the difficulty they had going through customs and finding a proper room at the hotel. But then at the end, she wrote that she hoped to see him soon.

I lowered the card, so he had not gone to Europe as the news article had said. He had stayed behind, but for how long? Had he eventually joined them or left his wife and child to remain behind at Whitehall Manor? I searched my mind for answers. There was only one reason to stay behind.

I flipped to the next postcard.

OCTOBER 1, 1921

Dearest Thomas,

What torments you? Why do you not leave Whitehall Manor and join us here in Paris as you promised? We've found the loveliest café. Little Georgie goes from fountain to fountain searching for coins while I work on attempting to paint. We have not heard from you in weeks. The last thing you said was that you were going to get your uncle from the hospital. How is the dear man? Has he recovered fully from the fire? If only you'd open up to me more. I know you sent us away so that you could help him get well. I remember you said you didn't want to burden me. How kind you are. So much like your mother. Brave and noble, but we can afford a caregiver for your uncle. Hire someone at once, a beautiful young nurse, and find your way to meet us here. We miss you so.

-Your Abigail

OCTOBER 15, 1921

Dearest Thomas,

It is such a disappointment that your uncle has passed away but now nothing can keep you from coming to join us on our next leg of the journey. We leave our hotel tomorrow morning and head toward the warmth of the southern Mediterranean next. How you must need the sun now that you've been through the heartbreak of tending to someone in their final hours.

We will get your ticket for the next tour. How Georgie misses you so, but not more than I do. Hurry soon to us, my dear.

-Your Abigail

NOVEMBER 3, 1921

Dearest Thomas,

It is really too much, my darling. Your last letter said you would book your ticket after the funeral, but the funeral must have passed and now you say you are consumed with repairs to the home, sealing up the old room in which your uncle slept. You said it was his childhood room and no longer needed. I don't understand you, my darling. How could a room not be needed? How do your changes to the house take priority over joining your family? I am reassured by your promises yet concerned by your ever-changing stories. Do you want to be with us or not? I have a good mind to return by the end of this month if I do not hear from you.

Deeply concerned,
Your Abigail

I LOWERED THE POSTCARDS. Thomas had brought J.B. Towry back to Whitehall Manor. He had lied to Abigail. He had told her he was his uncle but omitted to tell her the truth, that this man was also his father and the criminal who had killed his mother and siblings. Something had gone wrong. J.B. Towry had died soon after his arrival at Whitehall Manor. He had a funeral but no body had been put in the ground. Thomas then boarded up the spare room.

There was only one thing that could explain what happened next. My hands shook. Boarding up the spare room meant he was concealing something. Had he buried J.B. Towry's body in his childhood room? I felt a punch to the gut. The room that I had said would be the baby's room. I had to get down there and find the bones. But where? In the floorboards? In the walls? In the ceiling. I'd tear every part of the room apart to find them.

Just then, voices surfaced around me. I turned toward their direction, eyeing the vents. Following the sound to the furthest end of the attic, the sound grew louder nearest the corner beyond the wardrobe. That must be directly over the staff quarters. No longer were there holes in the flooring but there was what appeared to be an opening in the vent. I pressed my ear to it and heard Terran's voice.

"It's impossible," he said. "Anne is still unwell."

I didn't understand. I inched closer until I was nearly stepping into the insulation.

Another voice lifted to me. "We need to get rid of her. Anne is a cancer to Whitehall Manor. She will never understand us. She will never truly comprehend what love means. She's mad now."

"I worry she's becoming like her father. It's gotten even worse."

"Before too long, she'll be a raving lunatic. Maybe she'll even try to kill us."

"It's because her whole life she's been alone. She's turned her loneliness into insanity."

"Let us run away together then."

I strained again to see through the vent.

"No, I can't," Terran said. "Not with the baby on the way. There are a few weeks left now."

"A few weeks? Anne's not due until the end of August. That's six weeks away. I can't wait that long." Penelope stroked his cheek. "You must leave her now. The longer you wait, the worse it will be. Besides, she's bringing you down. She'll eventually destroy herself and everyone around her."

Terran turned his face toward hers. "If only I didn't feel so awful for her."

"Oh, but why? You didn't cause her to go insane. Do you know the other day she had me running around the house searching for more firewood for that endless fire of hers?"

"Oh, don't get me started on the fire."

"It's hotter than Hades in this house and in July of all months."

"I can't imagine what the air conditioning bill will be."

"And do you know what I saw her doing this morning? She was eating dirt from the garden, shoving whole handfuls in her mouth like it was chocolate cake."

"No, she didn't."

"She did, and what's worse is that I've found whole drawers full of dirt in her closet. She'd never want you to know, but I've seen her come into the house with her pockets full of it, leaving a trail wherever she goes that I have to clean up. Then, she puts the dirt in her closet wardrobe as if she's going to eat it later."

"I've tried to get her to see the doctor but she refuses.

There's nothing more that can be done." He pressed his lips to Penelope's.

When they pulled apart, Penelope whispered, "You have two choices. Either we run away tonight or we get rid of her."

My eyelids fluttered closed. It felt as if the world was collapsing around me. Inching even closer, I balanced against the floorboards, angling myself until at last, I could finally see fully down into the staff quarters. Terran sat on Penelope's bed. His hand was on top of hers as he brushed back her blond hair from her shoulder and kissed her neck.

I rolled back and muffled a sob. How could Terran do this to me? How could he possibly betray me like this? Yes, everything he said to Penelope was true. I was not used to showing love. I had lived alone for too long. I was damaged, but never did I think he would share my weaknesses with someone else. The two of them laughing at me was too much. And, with my housekeeper to make matters worse. And all the while, I had tried to keep them safe while they betrayed me. Their laughter rose again through the vents making me clench my fists.

If they wanted to get rid of me, they needed to get in line. I squared my shoulders. It was my unborn child that took precedence over them. I would do whatever it took to protect the baby. I hurried out of the attic. I knew where J.B. Towry's body was buried, and I was going to get rid of it.

CHAPTER

TWENTY-THREE

T he first swing into the floorboards was the hardest. I had found an ax, hammer, and crowbar in the toolshed and hauled them up to the baby's room.

The floors were over two hundred years old and untouched. It broke my heart to tear them apart but somewhere beneath these boards was J.B. Towry's body. The wood cracked as I swung and hit the plank again. When finally it relented I used the crowbar to pull back the first board. Sweat dripped down my back. The baby kicked furiously. I ached for a glass of water but there was no time.

I cracked the second and third boards removing several feet of planking so that I could look down beneath into what appeared to be a small space between the floor and the downstairs ceiling.

"What is happening?" Terran yelled as he came into the room. "What are you doing to the floors?"

Ignoring him, I shoved my head beneath and saw nothing but years of dust and mouse droppings. "It must be the other side of the room," I said, ignoring him. I turned and again swung the ax to the floorboard.

Terran tried to take the ax from me but I pulled back. "You will injure yourself and the baby. Please stop."

Penelope was next to rush into the room. She covered her mouth and stepped back.

I swung again. This time only inches from where Terran stood. The wood splintered. "If you want to help me, fine. If not, I suggest you leave. And take her." I hissed.

Terran went to Penelope and whispered something. She then turned and left.

My blood boiled. Did they think I was stupid? Instead of confronting them, I used my anger to pull up the floorboard. The nails cracked from their frames pinging to the other side of the room. Again, I searched beneath the boards for any sign of skeletal remains. There was nothing, but that was impossible.

Somewhere in this room had to be the body of J.B. Towry. It had to be this room. If not here, then where? I scanned the walls. Could it be that he was buried in the walls? Or the closet?

Heaving the ax over my shoulder, I leaned back and swung into the wall over the changing table.

"No!" Terran rushed to my side and forced the ax from my grip.

I wiped the sweat from my brow.

"I'm not going to let you destroy Whitehall Manor with this madness. What are you doing?"

"It's my house," I said. "If I don't like it, I can do whatever I want to it."

"What's really going on?" he demanded.

"He's in this house," I said. "His body is here. We have to find him before the baby is born."

Terran's face reddened. His nostrils flared. "I've had it with this delusion. You're going to be seen by the doctor."

"Where's Penelope?" I demanded. "Where's your new girlfriend?"

"What?"

I picked up the crowbar and shook it at him. "You heard me. I know what you've been doing. I heard you through the vents. I know you've been cheating."

He stared dumbfounded.

"Just as I thought. No words."

"I don't know what you're hearing in your head, but I'm not cheating on you."

"Lies." I moved toward the closet next. "Help me pull down the ceiling in here." My eye darted to something else. "There's an unusual mark on the wall. Maybe this is where his body was put."

Terran sighed. "Before you destroy everything we've spent a fortune restoring, have you thought maybe there's a better way to look for a body?"

I stepped from the closet. "What?"

"Detective Richards. He can be out here tomorrow. They have the equipment to search for bones."

"Fine," I said. "Call him."

Terran eased the crowbar from my hands and picked up the remaining tools. "It wouldn't hurt to wait one more day."

I gnawed on my thumb where a splinter had embedded. "Every day matters. We don't know when J.B. Towry will try again to force us from the house. And the baby will be here soon, Terran, in six weeks. We can't wait to rid the house of him."

"One more day, okay?"

Before I could object, Terran had left the room, locking the door behind him.

I rushed to the door, twisting the knob. "Let me out. Terran? Let me out. Let me out!" I spun back to the window. The hawk had returned and began to peck at the window. My god, I was too pregnant to attempt crawling out the window. Why had he locked me in the room?

There could only be one reason. He'd sent Penelope to call for the doctor. He'd be here soon. An hour at the most. What then? Would they force me into the hospital? I couldn't risk it. I had to find the body. There was still time. I would show them I wasn't insane. I would show them that the bones were somewhere in this room.

Not long after the rumbling sound of tires on the driveway pulled my attention up from the floor to the window where the pestering hawk had cracked the window. Beyond the bird, Dr. McCallister parked his car.

Penelope rushed out to meet him and pointed up to the window where I stood watching them. When she saw me, she turned away and hurried back inside. So, this was how they wanted it? They would try to say I was insane. Terran would try to take my baby.

A few minutes later, the door clicked open.

Dr. McCallister slowly walked into the room. His eyes grew larger as he examined the destruction. "Hello, Anne," he said. "Working on another renovation?"

"In a way," I said.

I heaved myself up from the rocking chair and resumed where I had left off, pulling up another floorboard. There had been no sense in waiting in vain, so while I sat locked in the room, I continued my work. The floorboards were mostly all removed now, revealing the framework beneath and the decades of dust that had been concealed. I used nothing but my hands to do it. My fingernails were torn from their beds. Splinters lined my palms. Blood dripped from my hands to the floor and was smeared across my forehead where I had wiped the sweat from my brow while digging into the walls of the closet.

"I think it might be good for the baby if you took a little rest," the doctor said.

"There's no time to rest. He'll be here soon."

"Who?"

"The ghost," I whispered. "J.B. Towry. He's coming for my baby."

Terran stood in the doorway along with Penelope, the two traitors.

Dr. McCallister turned to them and nodded.

They rushed over the floor's framework toward me and held me down while the doctor opened his medicine bag and pulled out a needle.

"Don't do this," I begged. "We don't have time for this. He'll be here soon. He'll be here!"

The doctor took his time jabbing the needle into a small glass vile.

I thrashed in their grip. "You traitors," I said. "You will kill all of us. Let me go."

There was no use. The doctor stepped toward me. He shoved the needle into my arm. My screams turned to whimpers. They finally let go. I wanted to collapse to the floor.

When I was half conscious, they moved me from the baby's room. "Don't take me to the attic," I mumbled.

"We wouldn't do that," Terran said.

"Don't put me up there and forget me."

"You're going for a rest," Dr. McCallister said. "No one is going to put you in the attic."

A few moments later, I was alone with Terran in the bedroom. He undressed me, closed the shades, and ordered Penelope to not come into this room under any circumstances.

I felt as if I could hear all the conversations in the house now. Penelope complained that Terran had waited too long to get me help. The doctor mentioned the words psychotic break and hospital admittance. Terran refused. He said he would stay and make sure I was looked after, but I didn't trust him. Oh, I didn't trust him at all to look after me. He was a cheater and a liar. He had promised to marry me and had said he loved me.

After a few minutes, the sedative the doctor gave me began to take hold of my thinking. It dulled the edges of my thoughts. I was at a hopeless loss for ever finding the bones. As I drifted off to sleep, J.B. Towry entered the room and took his seat in the corner.

He lit his pipe and laughed. My misery was his joy.

TWENTY-FOUR

I chewed my food slowly and stared out the window at the hazy sun. Two weeks had passed since my attempt to find where John Burton had been buried. A noise in the corner shifted my attention. Penelope sat where normally J.B. Towry watched me. How long had she been there?

"Good morning, Anne," she said, in a sweet voice as she eased from the chair.

Glancing in her direction, I felt sure she didn't wish me anything good. I glared at her and said, "I think I like the more formal way of doing things. Ms. Towry is fine."

"Of course, Ms. Towry," she said, her deception concealed by a pleasant smile. "I brought you a book to read." She placed it by my side. "The doctor said you're doing better now. Two weeks of rest has helped you."

I reached to pick it up, noticing the restraints on my wrists. How long had they been there? I examined her one more time then turned my attention to the door. "Where's Terran?"

"Gone into town."

My fists clenched as I thought of how I wished I could get her to leave me alone. "I know what's going on."

"What's that?" she asked.

"You're sleeping with my fiancée."

"Nothing is going on. It's in your head."

"I want you to leave," I said. "Leave Whitehall Manor right now. You're dismissed."

"Anne, Ms. Towry, please you're not well. I'll let you rest."

"Leave this house," I hissed. "You think I wouldn't find out?"

"Should I call for the doctor again?"

"No," I said, fighting against the restraints.

"Yes, I think that might be best. Another injection to calm your nerves."

"I'm not sick." I tried to kick her, but she quickly sidestepped, avoiding my foot. "That's what you want, isn't it? You want to have me institutionalized. You want me to be sent away, don't you?"

"No, Anne," she said. "I don't. I want you to fight whatever is haunting you. This curse you speak of. You need to fight it. I want you to be here for your baby."

For days after, I lay in bed, allowed only to use the restroom and read a book as needed. She brought me a new one from the library each day. A romance novel one day. A fantasy the next. A historical novel on the third day. Never a horror novel. Not even a mystery or thriller. Nothing to rattle my so-called fragile mind.

I rarely saw Terran now. Only at night. Before bed, Terran tightened my restraints, keeping me from moving from my bed while I spoke to the apparition of the gruesome man at my bedside. He whispered what he wanted to do to me and the baby. I felt his cold touch on my cheek, and long dirty nails slide down my neck to my chest and prod at my belly as if he could take it from me if he wanted. Then he smiled and laughed as he watched my face twist in horror.

It was Penelope who sat with me as I ate my meals, watching carefully how I used my fork. It became mostly Penelope who took care of me as the days crept into August. Terran had practically vanished, and I couldn't help but wonder if he had abandoned Whitehall Manor, me, and the baby.

The hot early-August sun made it unbearable to leave the window open. Large cicadas beat against the window panes while the air conditioning strained to keep up with the oppressive heat.

"Would you like me to bring you some ice cream for dessert this evening?" Penelope asked. "I know you like lemon. I could go to the store and get some."

"Is there no one else who could do that?"

"No," Penelope said.

Still Terran kept the staff at bay. No one was allowed at Whitehall Manor. I could only imagine what the gardens must look like with the overgrowth.

"Lemon is fine," I said.

She picked up my empty tray and began to make her way to the door.

"The restraints are very tight," I said. "Couldn't you loosen them a little?"

"The doctor said no. It's either this way or we have to take you to the hospital to be admitted."

I couldn't help but wonder if that would be better. Stay there until the baby was born but would that stop the ghostly visions of J.B. Towry or would that subdue me enough so that I could no longer see him? If I left, he would take over. It would be nearly impossible to resume control. Whitehall Manor would slip into a dark spell that would be impossible to break. No, I had to stay on my guard.

"Anything else?" Penelope asked.

She looked tired. Shadows had formed under her normally bright eyes, and I knew it must be from the late nights with my fiancée. How I hated her and wished she'd leave. I wished things could go back to how they were before when we had no money, and it was just Terran and I and the house.

She left the room. Around me, there was silence, the still of the mid-morning, but I knew J.B. Towry was somewhere nearby, somewhere lurking. I turned my engagement ring with my thumb as I tried to make sense of it. I had torn apart the baby's room, put holes into the closet, and ripped apart the walls, but nothing.

If only I could get Detective Richards to help me. I had to get a note to him. I reached for the book Penelope brought me to tear out a sheet of paper from the front and dug through the nightstand for a pen. I would write the note and convince Penelope to deliver it for me. I would pay her with my jewelry. If she could be so easily convinced to cheat, then I could convince her to help me. I had such lovely jewelry passed down from my mother. I knew beneath those angelic eyes she was like the rest of us.

I opened the book when suddenly a note fell into my lap. I stared at it for a moment. The book was old, from the early nineteen hundreds, a Highlands romance novel that I never intended to read, but the note. I slowly opened it and scanned the words.

My heart thudded in my chest. I flipped to the last page

to see it was written by Thomas Towry. A letter to his wife tucked away in the book from the library. I took a breath. But how? I scanned the other pages of the book. There were no other notes. I couldn't waste another moment, so I quickly started to read.

CHAPTER
TWENTY-FIVE

O ctober 24, 1923

To My Beloved,

I must write this letter to you with the hope that you will understand my decision in the coming days. I had not envisioned anything like this would come to pass but it has. I am beyond tormented by the wickedness of my uncle. I will tell you what happened over the last two years and try my best to explain my choices. Although the events may seem illogical and possibly delusional, they are nonetheless true.

It started long before the fire burned down the Sanatorium in Baltimore. It began before I was born. The trigger of catastrophic events began the day J.B. Towry was conceived. He is an evil, spiteful man who cannot be changed but he is not to be blamed for my selfish choices. They were my own. They were my undoing. Pride and obstinate determination have run through

177

the Towry blood for generations. It was this arrogance that blinded me to what I will tell you next.

My part in this began when I received an urgent telegram from the doctors at the asylum requesting direction as to where my uncle should be taken. My first thoughts were of our son. He had never known the tortures that I had. He had not known what it was like to suffer without knowing his mother or live far away from my home with people who barely wanted him. I thought of how Caroline had suffered for twenty long years, the ten children she'd given birth to because of J.B. Towry's repeated assaults, and the nine children who lay dead in the fields and gardens of Whitehall Manor. All but me.

As I was told before by my great aunt who never let me forget one minute of the wicked Towry's madness, my uncle was found bloodied and sick in his bedroom at Whitehall Manor in late spring of 1881. Having contracted malaria, J.B.'s already sickened mind had grown delirious as he descended the cellar steps to abuse my mother once again. In his weakened state, Caroline took the opportunity to escape.

She fought him off as she had many times before. Caroline was no longer the bright-eyed, ambitious young woman she had been when this torment began. She was nearly forty years old, sickened from lack of sunshine and proper nutrition, a practical skeleton that lived on whatever J.B. threw to her over the years, an uncooked piece of pig flesh, a half-eaten corn cob, or a worm-riddled apple. She drank water from the leak in the trap door but there had been times when it didn't rain for a week and in the early days she nearly died from thirst until she learned to collect water in mason jars and survive with the wretched stench of herself that was only taken away once a month by my uncle.

But on the day of her freedom, she fought with what strength she had left and climbed the stairs of the cellar toward the sun.

Against all odds, my mother survived to give birth to me. What kept her going in the following weeks is a mystery. By all means, Caroline should have given up long ago.

Claw marks along the trapdoor from repeated attempts to break through were found by the men who investigated this crime. Slash marks along her wrists that had bled and healed multiple times told another story. It was said in the brief time that she lived following her escape, that she retold the events including her decision to stop fighting and lay in the darkness of the cellar to die but death refused to take her.

Even when J.B. opened the hatch letting the bright sun descend on her, she didn't have hope of pushing past him, cutting him with the glass she had cut herself with, or outwitting him by showing she could be trusted. There was simply no means of escape until one day when he tumbled down the stairs, sweating like a pig, coughing violently, and shaking.

Caroline could hardly believe he was still alive. His skin was ashen gray. His eyes were as blood red as the late autumn sun. His breath emitted a smell of evil so wicked she thought she would faint merely by being near him.

It is said that he panted the words, "You will die."

My mother was no longer affected by his threats. Death was a welcome place that long since made broken promises to her. She slowly stood. He reached out a hand to grab her ankle, locking his grip around her where only last week she had been chained. He had forgotten to lock it and she knew then he had the beginnings of some kind of delirium more robust than what she had seen before.

She worked on his fingers for a long time, pulling them apart, then feeling them tighten again. His breath was labored. Sweat dripped down his temples. Then, as if by miracle, he went unconscious, and his grip loosened.

Caroline wasted no time. She slowly stood feeling the ache in her bones and back and crawled toward the cellar stairs. She gazed up at the sun and smelled the fresh air and blossoms. She had forgotten what the world was like. Step by step, she ascended until at last, she was on level ground. She sank her fingers in the dirt and looked around her at the willow trees blowing in the gentle breeze and the oak tree leaves shimmering in the sun.

My mother made it only a half mile down the road away from Whitehall Manor before a man driving a T-Ford slammed on his brakes and stared aghast at the ghostly figure wandering away from Whitehall Manor. I can only imagine what horrors must have passed through that man's mind as he saw my mother bleeding from between her legs, a vacant stare in her eyes, and two skeleton arms reaching out for help.

She was taken to the local hospital where I was born prematurely at eight months. I was severely ill and stayed in the hospital for almost a year, at which time my mother died. I can only say that it was a blessing she died in a clean bed and not beneath the ground of Whitehall Manor.

As for my uncle, he was also discovered that same day Caroline was. He had regained consciousness and crawled back to the house to die, but he was found by the local sheriff and not long after his terrible crime was exposed, he was taken immediately to the sanatorium, the state refusing to press charges against someone so clearly insane.

The bodies of the babies were discovered, at least most of them, and cremated as the medical examiner said they were too beyond recognition in some circumstances to ever allow for burial. The ashes were spread in Willow Creek.

For eighteen years, I lived without my mother and when I grew older, I was told the circumstances of my existence. My uncle was also my father. I grew angry at what J.B. Towry had done to Caroline and my siblings. I kept the anger buried deep *and decided instead to pour forth my energy into improving the Towry name.*

The telegram from the hospital woke something in me that I thought was long since dead. I felt there was little time left. J.B. Towry was in his eighties. I needed to hear him beg for forgiveness. I needed to see him accept his crimes. I decided at that moment to send you and little Georgie away to Europe. I had no other choice but to lie to you. I was trying to protect you from the monster that had lived in me for so long and that I knew was emerging.

Once you and Georgie were gone and the staff had been told to not return, I picked up J.B. Towry from the Red Cross shelter they had erected only down the street from the nearly destroyed Sanatorium. My uncle was now in a wheelchair. He was eighty-three years old and spent most of his time staring past me with drool forming at the sides of his mouth.

The nurse at the station asked if I had arranged help for him at Whitehall Manor. I told her that I had but knew help would not be necessary.

Upon returning home, I noticed a slight shift in his demeanor. He lifted his chin and scanned the house as if seeing it for the first time. I knew from what I had been told that his determination to take over the property was still strong. He had no claim to it, however. Only my mother Caroline did and before her death when I was only one month old, she had her will written to pass the entire fortune on to me. My uncle never succeeded in his mission to destroy her.

With the house to myself, I took my uncle-father from the car and lowered him into the wheelchair. The house was not suitable for wheelchairs. There was no way to get him up the stone steps, so instead, I pushed him through the grass, around the side of the house.

Outside the doors that led to the sitting room, I took him from his chair and lifted him inside. He must have weighed less than one hundred pounds, a shocking sight for what I had been told was once a strong military prospect who stood six foot three and weighed more than two hundred pounds in his prime.

After lowering him into the chair beside the hearth, I sat across from him examining his lined face, wondering how such a pathetic man as this could ever have frightened anyone, and wondered if he even remembered his crimes toward my mother.

He stared at me through clouded eyes.

My resentment grew. It pulsed in me as I stood from the chair and paced the room yelling obscenities directed at him. I called him a coward, a liar, and a murderer. All of which was true. The more I cursed and ranted, the more rage I felt surface in me until finally I found myself standing with the fire poker in one hand and J.B. Towry's unconscious body at my feet.

I had struck him in a blackout rage. Blood trickled from the corner of his upturned lips. Had he been laughing at me? Was that what finally drove me to madness?

The poker clattered to the ground as I pulled my uncle up by the lapels of his jacket. I stared into his half-dead eyes. It was then I fell under some kind of spell in which I could hear his voice though his lips did not move.

He wanted me to kill him. He begged for his death. I was more than happy to comply. I let his old body fall to the ground and again I picked up the fire poker and bashed his skull.

The rage that had dwelled inside of me for decades emerged in full force. I, the representative of my lost brothers and sister, the defender of my mother's name, struck him over and over again until his brains spilled out onto the floor.

His legs twitched and then everything stopped. I was beating a corpse for a great deal of time after the man who had occupied it long since expired.

I stumbled back to the chair by the fire, dropped the poker, and placed a hand over my beating heart. It was my fault that he was dead. I had brought him back to Whitehall Manor knowing that this rage burned inside of me. I had killed a man, my uncle, and my father. I held my head and rocked back and forth and moaned.

If only the story ended there. But it didn't. At some point in the night, I heard J.B. Towry's voice around me. I heard the echoes of his thoughts. They consumed me and drove me to what I will tell you next.

Oh, think kindly of me when I tell you this next part. Remember me for my goodness and as a kind father to Georgie. It was beyond my ability to comprehend but I was drawn back to the dead man's body. I laid my ear on his chest and heard his heart thudding in his chest. He had not died. Despite his head crushed on the floor, his heart still beat.

Sickened and mad, I rushed to find a knife and hurried back to the room. I plunged it into his chest, cutting open his flesh and breaking open his ribcage, exposing what could not be. Before me, his heart beat black in his chest. Its loud pulsing consumed my thoughts as I cut it from his body and stared at it in my hand. How it still beat, I could not tell you. I was confused and delusional. I was past the point of madness. I had sunk into total and complete insanity. My thoughts turned to hiding the body. I had to get rid of it before I lost everything.

The woodsmoke would conceal the scent of his decaying body. If only I could throw him in his grave or toss him into Willow Creek, but what if a medical inquisition occurred? What if his body surfaced? They would see immediately from his crushed skull how he met his end and a floating body in the water wouldn't be any better.

There was no other choice. I would have to burn his body in the hearth. I added wood to the fire until it smoked like the heat of hell. The ten-foot hearth easily fit his whole body, but the five-

foot grate on which his body rested was hardly big enough. What was left of his head dangled off the edge of the grate as the rest of the body caught fire. The body popped and smoldered. The putrid smell of burning flesh filled my nose and made me vomit more than a few times. The roasted flesh from J.B. Towry's face melted, dripping chunks of skin and flesh that sizzled in the fire, leaving nothing but his fractured skull.

For days after, I kept the fire blazing, burning hot until the bones began to crack under the heat. All the while, the black heart of his continued to beat. What didn't burn came under the hammer as I smashed the bits and pieces of what was left of his bones. Then, finally scooping the remains into a bucket, I carried them to Willow Creek and spread them deep off the dock.

For what reason I did not burn the heart is this. In the early morning hours as the sun began to lift over the tree line of Willow Creek and reveal a glow of pink hues, I felt a part of me that still clung to humanity. It was a thread of such thinness that it might snap at any moment but the heart in my hands was the last of the connection. I held the last of my father and could not destroy his heart while it still beat strong.

Instead, I took it and placed it in a metal box. This would have to be hidden. Once the fire burned out, I shifted the grate and opened the ash pit, placing it below the fireplace, in the small hole that would go undetected.

My darling, forgive me, but I could not admit then to what I had done. I knew that murder was an act of pure evil and now I had allowed it into my soul. I tried desperately to conceal my tracks. I held a funeral and buried an empty coffin in the Towry cemetery. I told the hospital J.B. Towry had not survived the journey home and they accepted the news with some relief.

His voice followed me and in a desperate attempt to end it, I sealed-up his childhood room. Even the sight of the room made me physically ill. I knew it was where his spirit returned upon his death when it was not following me through the house and gardens.

In a panic, I ran from my crimes and joined you in Europe where I thought my horrendous deeds would not follow me, and for a time they did not, but upon our return to Whitehall Manor, I thought of nothing else. The heart beneath the hearth thudded in time with my own from dawn to dusk.

Every time I passed the sealed-up room, I shivered. When I took the boat out on the water, I felt his presence around me. His voice lingered in my ear. His threats of eternal damnation and death to my son closed in. No matter what I did I could not stop him. What made matters worse, was his ability to possess me as I frequently found myself in rooms of the house not knowing how or why I got there.

As time went on, he improved his control of me. I wakened in the attic one day without knowing how I got there, a knife held to my throat by my own hand as I stared into the wardrobe mirror. If not for our son's voice calling to me, I'm sure J.B. Towry would have dragged the knife across my neck and laughed as I bled to death.

Even now, J.B. Towry's whispers continue to haunt me at night while we sleep. He threatens to kill both of you. I know now what I must do. There's only one choice. You and Georgie must leave. You must leave and go to your mother's home and never return. This is my doing. I must face the consequences as I foolishly thought I could correct the problem but know there's no hope. J.B. Towry speaks to me. His thoughts worm once again into my head. He tells me the noose has been prepared. Soon, I will fall under his possession. There is no hope for me. There is no stopping him. By dusk I will be dead.

Goodbye, my love. Protect our child with every ounce of your soul. I have become yet another victim of the Towry curse. My weakness was my hope. Now, there is none. I dare not go near the beating heart and beg you to stay away from it as well.

Runaway tonight! Flee for your lives! Do not return! Do not look back! This of you I beg.

Yours truly,
Thomas Towry

TWENTY-SIX

"What's that?" The sound of Terran's voice pulled me from my thoughts.

I sat up in my bed, lowering the letter to my lap, finally understanding what had happened. Thomas's letter explained why he brought J.B. Towry back to Whitehall Manor. It explained why he committed suicide. Most importantly, it told me how to end the curse.

Terran stood by the window. "You don't want to tell me. That's fine. I know you're mad at me. The least I deserve is the silent treatment."

"Will you loosen the restraints? I have to use the bathroom."

"In a moment," he said. "I want to talk about what the doctor said."

I kicked off the blankets. "There's no sense in talking about it."

"You have less than a month until the baby is born. The doctor said the delusions and hysteria may be brought on by hormonal changes or even a prior mental illness that has been aggravated by your pregnancy, but after the baby is born, he said things may get better."

I knew things would get worse. The baby would be out in the world, more vulnerable than ever, but I said nothing.

"If you can hold on one more month. I know it's been horrible. You will see more clearly then that nothing is going on between Penelope and me. This is a manifestation of your paranoia."

"I want what's best for the baby," I said, not lying.

"Me too." He rushed to my side and embraced me, smoothing back my hair and kissing my cheeks and lips. "I want what's best for both of us, our family, our home.

If only I could convince him that I wanted the same, but he couldn't see what I saw. He couldn't know what I knew. "Please, Terran, loosen my restraints. Let's be kind to each other. I have loved you from the moment I saw you. Please, I need you. Please say you still love me."

"I do love you," he said as his hand caressed my cheek, the same way I saw him caress Penelope's.

"Should we go for our walk this morning?" he asked.

"I would like that."

He loosened the restraints and helped me get washed and changed then together we walked down the stairs out the side door and into the gardens.

The late afternoon cicadas hummed. It had been over two weeks since I'd been outside. My soul needed it. I took a deep breath and gazed across the land. The green grass had dried brown in the sun. Without the gardeners, the land had begun to return to its primitive state. The cattails near the waterfront multiplied. The soft loamy soil slid between my toes. Tree limbs hung close to the ground and the hedges overgrew at strange angles.

"I've done my best to keep the garden alive," he said,

"but you'll need to get better. We need help. We have to show the staff that it's safe to return."

I nodded, wanting the same as him. I couldn't help but wonder what had changed. For two weeks he barely showed himself and now he was worried about me or was it that he was worried about his prospects at Whitehall Manor? How had we drifted so far apart? We both loved the same things. There was only one answer.

"Where's Penelope?" I asked.

"Gone to get you ice cream," he said.

"She's very considerate." I made my way to a particularly lovely marigold, pulling its head from the stem and crushing it in my grip as he continued discussing his plans for the next few weeks.

"It's not that I want you to stay in bed. The doctor said it would be best. He wants as little stress for you as possible."

"Do I look stressed now?" I asked.

"No, you look wonderful." Again, he leaned in and kissed me. "I do love you, Anne. And I love our baby."

We lingered in the Marigold Garden for a while longer as I tried desperately to piece together the information I had figured out about J.B. Towry. It was a near-impossible task with my mind feeling heavy from the sedation. Trying to string my thoughts together was a constant struggle.

"Do you want to go back?" Terran asked, noticing me shiver.

"I wonder if it would be okay to sit by the fire today."

"No, Anne. The old routines are over. No more sitting by the fire. No more staring into the fire. No more hoarding dirt."

"I've not hoarded dirt."

He ran a shaky hand through his hair. "Every drawer in the bedroom is full of it."

"I don't remember doing that." I wanted to explain that it couldn't have been me, but I didn't know for sure.

"I should get you back to bed."

I reached for his hand and stepped close to him, kissing him deeply. I had to get Terran on my side. I had to get him to understand that the threat to the baby was real. I needed time to understand how to keep us safe.

He guided me back to the house and up through the garage and east wing staircase to our bedroom.

"Why don't you try to rest?" As he reached for the restraints, his eyes fell on the letter next to the bed. "What is this?"

"It was from my great-grandfather," I said. "It explains everything. I know you don't want to hear me talk about this but it's true."

His eyes scanned the letter. When he was done, he looked back at me. "Why did you do this?"

"What do you mean?"

"Why did you write this?"

"I didn't," I said. "It came from the book you brought me. It fell out of the book."

"Anne, it didn't fall out of the book. It's a page from the book. Look." He showed me the torn edges that lined up with the first page of the novel. "You ripped a blank page and wrote on it."

"I did not," I said, my eyes widening. "That's impossible. Everything in that letter lines up with the truth. My great-grandfather killed J.B. Towry. He burned his body in the hearth. It says that. That letter is his message to his wife before he killed himself."

"You wrote it," he said, reaching for the pen beside me.

My mouth fell open. I could only stare for a moment as I tried to figure out what was happening.

"Look, Anne. Look." Terran held up the letter.

The red pen was the same shade as the words written in the letter, but the handwriting wasn't my own. "I-I don't know what to say."

"It's all a part of your disorder. I don't understand it myself." He stood and tore the letter in two and dropped it in the trash. "Maybe you wanted answers to what happened at the charity event and to explain what happened to your grandfather but you can't conjure up explanations. Sometimes bad things happen. That's all."

"No," I said, shaking my head. I felt hot tears sting my cheeks as I covered my face with my hands.

He pulled me to him and let me cry on his shoulder.

"I'm wrong," I said, moaning. "Oh, I've made your life miserable. I've made this house an asylum. I did this, all of this, but why?"

"It's okay," he said, smoothing back my hair and kissing my cheeks. "You've had a lot of stress since your parents died. It was all too much. It was your mind trying to make sense of it. But everything will be okay now. This is good." He pulled back. "You now see what you're doing. Oh, Anne. I need you. I need you."

I needed him, too. Between kisses, I found my hands holding his face and pulling him to me. I slipped out of my nightgown. My breasts had grown heavy in the last month and my belly was large and swollen but I didn't care.

"You look beautiful," he said, placing his hand on my stomach. "More beautiful than ever."

He pulled off his shirt. The musky scent of his body awakened me. I needed him desperately. Sweat glistened from his brow. I moaned as his lips traveled to my breasts, cupping each one as he caressed me. My fingers found their way through his hair pulling him toward me as he fumbled to take off his pants. A moment later he pushed inside of me. I moaned and clung to him. My passion was ignited for the first time in months. If only we could stay like this forever. Waves of pleasure washed over me. His eyes closed as he pushed deeper into me, cradling my head between kisses.

We lay there in the warmth of the afternoon as the rays of the sun pushed through the blinds onto his tanned skin until his body relaxed and his soft snores filled the room. I loved Terran more than anything in the world. I wanted our relationship to work. I couldn't understand my mind. I couldn't grasp that I had been so wrong when I always prided myself on my strong instincts.

As I draped myself in my silk robe and eased from the bed, I knew there was one way for sure to prove that Terran and the doctors were right. I needed to look beneath the hearth.

I hurried quickly from the room, downstairs, and into the sitting room. They had let the fire go out while I lay bedridden and restrained upstairs, but that would help me now as I opened the screen and laid it to the side.

Weeks' worth of ash lay on the pit cover. I would soon be covered in it myself, but there was no other option. Just as I reached to shift the grate, the sound of the front door opening and closing echoed behind me. I gasped and tried to shift everything back into place as Penelope entered the room.

"What are you doing in here?" Penelope said as she came into the sitting room. She shifted her sunglasses to the top of her head and dropped the keys on the side table as if she were walking into her own home. "The fire? Are you starting that again? Don't you think it's hot enough?"

"Not quite," I said.

"Does Terran know you're here?"

"Yes, he's resting." I sat in the chair. "We just made love. I wore him out and he'd like to be left alone."

She stayed quiet for a moment as I examined her reaction. She clucked her tongue and then said, "I'll put the ice cream away before it melts."

When she stepped from the room, I turned and quickly pulled out the grate again. I grabbed the fire brush and swept away the debris. Beneath the blackened pile was a trapdoor, an ash pit. I tried to dig my nails into its edges but there was nothing left of them. I grabbed the tongs, knocking down the whole stand of equipment that clanged to the floor, and tried to pry open the sides. It took a moment, but finally, I managed to open it. I pulled back the heavy steel lid and reached down into the opening.

"What on earth are you doing, Ms. Towry?" Penelope's voice called out.

I slid back. My hands were blackened from the ash. The floor beside me, too, and everything I touched. My eyes watched hers as she curiously studied me. I knew she'd texted Terran. She'd alerted him to my escape from the bedroom. A sheepish smile replaced her normal coquettish one.

"I should get you a wash cloth," she said, heading past me toward the bathroom.

"Please leave this house," I said to her. "We are all in danger."

"Uh, huh? What's that door you have opened beneath the grate?"

"The ash pit. It was where they used to sweep the ashes."

I needed her to leave the room. If only she would go back to the staff quarters and let me resume my search but before I could say another word the sound of Terran's feet thudding through the adjacent rooms neared.

"I don't think you need to do any more cleaning today, Ms. Towry," Penelope said as she stepped to the fireplace, kicked the ash pit door closed, and shifted the grate back into place. Just as Terran entered the room, she stood and said, "I think Ms. Towry needs her rest. Why don't I take her back to her bedroom."

CHAPTER
TWENTY-SEVEN

"Anne, you need to get back to your room," Terran said.

"No, I'm feeling much better. I think I'll sit here a little while longer."

"No, that's against the doctor's orders," Penelope said.

I slowly stood. "Terran, I want Penelope dismissed from Whitehall Manor right away. I've already fired her but she refuses to leave. Will you escort her from the premises?"

Terran glanced at the floor and said, "I don't think that's a good idea right now."

"Why?"

When he didn't say anything, I decided our lovemaking only a short time before meant nothing. He wasn't willing to part with Penelope. He allowed her to stay at Whitehall Manor and further divide us. It was clear he wasn't the strong man I needed but I said nothing. Instead, I glanced at my hands and said, "I'll go get cleaned up."

Penelope smiled as I passed her.

"I'll take my dinner in my room tonight," I said to her.

"Assuming you're still the housekeeper and not the lady of the manor."

"No, Ms. Towry. I'm your humble servant."

Terran led me back to the bedroom. As I got into the bed, he replaced the restraints.

"Don't do this," I begged. "You know you don't want to do this. I'm your fiancé. Please."

"It's not about that," he said, pushing a strand of hair from my face. "You need to rest," he said, closing the shades. "It won't be long. Once the baby is born, everything will be back to normal."

"Will we be back to normal?" I asked.

"I hope so, Anne." He went to the bathroom and brought back a washcloth, smoothing it over my hands and face. "I need you to get better."

"Will you go to her tonight? After you've been with me?"

"No," he said. "You need to rest. Don't overexert yourself."

When he left the room, I felt an overwhelming sense of worry descend upon me. I pressed my cheek into the pillow. Tears slipped to the soft cushioning. I had been so close to finding out what was true. My hands had touched something in the ash pit, but what? I didn't know for sure. There hadn't been enough time. I tugged at my restraints desperate to get back down there.

"Knock, knock," Penelope's voice came from the bedroom door. In her hands was the dinner tray I had requested. "I figured you'd want dinner now since you looked a little tired downstairs. Maybe an early night will help set you straight." She laid the tray on the bed.

On it was a sandwich on rye bread, a small salad from the garden, and the lemon ice cream she had promised. It did look delicious, but I could hardly eat now. I had to figure out how to get out of the restraints.

"Go on and eat your food," she said, picking up the washcloth and tidying up the room.

I watched her carefully. She picked up Terran's underwear he had left on the floor and pursed her lips. After a few minutes of cleaning up, she sat in the corner chair, watching me.

"There's no reason for you to stay," I said. "I obviously can't get out of these restraints."

She smiled and reached across to the table next to the chair, opening a small drawer, and pulling out a small box of colored cigarettes. I felt my stomach twist as she lit one and leaned back.

"Oh, you don't mind, do you? I figure since I'm more family now than staff that I should be allowed a few indulgences from time to time."

"By indulgences do you mean my fiancé?"

She laughed and gazed at her cigarette. "The best tobacco comes straight from the fields, wouldn't you agree?"

"I don't smoke."

"You're right. It's a horrible habit." She put the cigarette out on the side table beside the other mark from months ago. "Do you want me to leave?"

"Yes," I said. "I don't like being watched. Not when I'm awake and not when I'm asleep."

"Fine," she said, shifting to the edge of the chair. "I'll leave but first you have to eat some of your ice cream. I went to great lengths to find it for you. Three different stores."

I picked up the spoon and took a bite. It was wonderful.

Smooth and silky. I could eat a whole gallon of it. I devoured it within seconds.

"Do you suppose you could do without me?" she asked, slowly standing. "If I left, who would bring you your dinner or clean up after you? I thought about what you said. I thought about leaving. I had my bag packed not long after you lost your mind tearing up the baby's room. I thought I couldn't handle staying here with your lunacy for another day. But Terran needed me. If I left, he'd be alone with you."

"He won't leave me," I said. "We love each other."

"Maybe, but after you're gone, he'll forget you."

I shifted back in the bed. "What do you mean?"

"I think Whitehall Manor isn't good for you. I think it would be best if you left."

Staring at her, I said, "You don't know what you're saying. You don't know what's happening here."

"I think I do. I've been doing everything for you for months. Planning your charity event, looking after Terran while you went on your delusional adventures, cleaning and cooking with no one else to help me, and not even getting paid for all of it."

"Penelope, I-I may have forgotten. I'm sorry. I'll pay you now. I'll double your pay. But listen to me. You must leave now."

"No, that time has passed. I've decided I'm entitled to much more than a paycheck. Over the last few weeks, I've realized that Terran wants me. He sees you've gone mad. He worries about the baby. Well, that baby will be born and once you've gone off the deep end and killed yourself, it will be your child who inherits Whitehall Manor. I will be here to comfort him. He will fall in love with me. I will be a better wife and mother than you could ever be."

As she spoke an ache in my side began to radiate

through me. "I'm not going to kill myself, Penelope. I'm not going anywhere. It's you who is delusional."

She laughed. "Maybe you will. Maybe you'll have no other choice."

Her angelic eyes transformed in front of me and I knew then I was dealing with something much more sinister than I knew. Was I talking to J.B. Towry? I shivered and cringed in pain. She rushed to my side and pulled up the blanket.

"Oh, there, there," she said. "You must be going into early labor. That can happen sometimes."

"What?" I searched her eyes. They darkened before me.

She picked up the tray. "I would call for the doctor but I don't think he'll come out this late."

"Please, Penelope. Get Terran. You have to help me. I can't give birth alone."

She stared off for a moment then her voice changed. In a lower voice, that of a man, that of J.B. Towry, she said, "I think nine months is far too long to wait for a child. Eight months is better. Get it out of you. Hurry it along. I always believed that nature found its way to get rid of the weakest beings, the ones injured or hurt. Sometimes they crawl beneath a bush and die. Sometimes they're eaten by a hungry predator, but the world always rights itself, doesn't it?"

I stared in horror as the outline of her face took on the strong jaw of J.B. Towry, the beady eyes and the red-pallored skin tone. There was no doubt that he possessed her now. In a deep and dark voice, she turned a cold eye to me and said, "Then it will be our time for some fun."

CHAPTER

TWENTY-EIGHT

T writhed in pain. I tore at the bedsheets and screamed. The dull ache that started along my side intensified until it felt as if waves were crashing down on me, drowning me in an agony so deep I thought I'd never survive it.

The evening sun set and the darkness in the room surrounded me along with the wicked smell of J.B. Towry. I knew he waited in the corner to take my child from me. I was powerless to stop him and screamed again.

I felt myself in and out of pain and in and out of consciousness. "It's too soon," I said. Eight months is too soon. Fighting my way between contractions, I managed to take off my underwear but continued to battle against the restraints that kept me from getting help.

My mind filled with horrific images of my baby. It would be born deformed and twisted like Caroline's children, or worse yet, it would be born dead. Another contraction. I arched my back and screamed, gripping the restraints.

Then suddenly, the door flung open and Terran rushed

into the room. His gaze fell on me naked in bed, my legs opened, as I twisted back and forth. He came to my side and quickly loosened the restraints.

"Where have you been?" I yelled.

"I left. Penelope said you were fine. I heard your screams from the garden."

I moaned and gripped his hand until it turned red.

His faced contorted in pain.

When the contraction ended, he said, "We have to get you to the hospital."

"There isn't time."

"Then I'll call for the doctor." He pulled out his phone.

"The baby is coming now," I said, sitting up and positioning myself.

"You can't have the baby here. I don't know what to do. We need help."

I pulled him to me. "Penelope gave me something in my food. She's probably been putting it in every meal all week. She induced my labor."

"No," he said. "It's the stress. Everything you've put yourself through."

"For once will you please believe me?"

His eyes searched mine as Penelope walked into the room.

"Terran, this is women's work," she said. "Why don't you come away and let me handle this?"

He swallowed. "No, I'm staying. She needs me."

Her sweet face transformed before us.

"Get her out of the room," I said. "Lock the door."

Terran slowly stood as Penelope pulled out a sharp knife from behind her back.

"What are you doing?" he said.

Penelope smiled. "I was thinking that natural child

birth takes so long. Why not cut the bastard out? Then, we can be done with all this right now."

"You need to leave," he said to her as she raised the knife and slashed in his direction. He leaped back in time to avoid the blade.

Another contraction. I screamed and writhed in pain.

The scent of tobacco lingered in the room.

Penelope stepped toward me and Terran intercepted her wrist as she swung to stab me in the stomach. He pushed her back against the wall. The knife clanged to the ground. Then, he turned her around and dragged her to the door, throwing her into the hallway, and locking the door.

"Terran." I reached out a hand.

"Yes, sweetheart." He kissed my forehead. "The baby is coming. It will all be over soon. Keep pushing."

He helped me to sit up. I gritted my teeth and bore down feeling my lower half tear beneath me. I screamed in agony and fell back to the pillow covered in sweat.

Terran continued to move from my side to my lower half checking on the fast progress. He rushed to the bathroom and gathered blankets and towels then forced open the window to air out the smoke. When he returned to my side, he pressed a cold washcloth to my forehead between contractions.

"I can't do this on my own," I cried.

"You don't have to," he said.

The sound of scratching nails outside the bedroom door temporarily distracted me.

"It's not her," I said to him. "It's not Penelope. She's possessed."

"I saw her eyes change. She looked like a different person."

"It's him. It's J.B. Towry. You have to keep her from

taking the baby. If she gets her hands on it—" I sat up again and screamed as another contraction came on without warning.

Terran rushed to the end of the bed. As his eyes focused on the space between my legs, his face paled and he began to tremble. "Head's out," he whispered.

I reached down to feel. I touched a full head of hair. "Dark hair?"

"Yes," he said.

Fists pounded at the door. The lock rattled and I knew it was only a matter of time before she found her way in. The wind blew through the drapes and gave me some relief. I sat up again and on the next contraction, pushed, holding my hands down and feeling my child ease into my hands.

Terran remained silent until finally on my last push our child was born. I fell back to the pillows, holding my child on my stomach, crying as I examined his head, body, legs, and feet. He was perfect.

Then, suddenly the baby cried.

Terran embraced both of us. We were wet with tears.

The pain vanished just as the door suddenly broke from its lock, swinging open to reveal Penelope charging toward us with an ax raised over her head.

Terran pulled us away. The blade of the ax cut into the mattress only inches from where I had just been. I tumbled to the floor, cradling the baby in my arms. A plume of feathers burst into the air.

Again, the fight continued. Blow for blow, Penelope was infused with an intensity I didn't think she was capable of. She held one end of the ax in each hand and used it to punch Terran in the jaw.

He stumbled back to the ground.

She laughed. She swung back and brought the blade down again.

He rolled to his side. It cut into the wood floor and stuck there.

She worked on pulling it free and Terran lunged toward her shoving her to the ground. The knife she had first brought into the room slid across the floor toward me.

I tried desperately to get to my feet but couldn't. Another wave of pain passed through me as I climbed back into the bed. I gripped the headboard and pushed again, feeling myself deliver the placenta. The baby screamed beside me on the bed. Every instinct in me forced me to stand. I searched for the knife on the floor and used it to cut the umbilical cord.

The two fought, struggling for control. Terran punched her. She seemed to feel nothing and returned the blow to his face.

Knocked to the ground, she leaped on his back and pulled his head back exposing his neck. She turned her wicked face to me and said, "Give me the knife."

I shook my head. "Leave him alone." I picked up the baby, clutching him to my chest as Terran twisted away from her tight grip and kicked her back across the room.

"Anne, take the baby. Run!" Terran yelled.

"I won't leave you," I said.

Just then, Penelope got to her feet, a red rage pulsed in her face as she screamed and rushed toward Terran who stood before the opened window.

"Terran!" I cried out, turning away.

A shrill scream echoed around me. I felt myself shudder. When I turned back, Terran stood by the open window gazing down.

He faced me. His eyes were wide. Sweat coated his brow as he stuttered. "S-she fell."

I slipped on my robe and forced myself from the bed despite the pain and burning. I hurried to the window. I looked down to see Penelope's body. Her eyes stared back at me. Her neck was twisted at a strange angle exposing bone. Beneath her a pool of blood began to expand. An instant death once she hit the patio below.

"I killed her," Terran said. "But she attacked me. What happened? What's going on?"

I didn't have time to help him understand. Instead, I grabbed the blanket and wrapped the baby. "We have to get out of here. Now."

He stood by the window still staring at the dead woman.

"Don't you see? Penelope didn't go mad. I didn't go crazy. There's a ghost and it will come for you next. It will use you to kill me and the baby. He's going to possess one of us next. He's going to try and kill our child."

Tears flooded his eyes. He kissed the baby's head and then mine. He slowly nodded. "Let's get out of here."

He helped me slip on my shoes and leave the room. Every part of my body hurt. All I wanted to do was stay in bed but I couldn't.

As we made our way into the hall, the house seemed to groan. Whispers surrounded me. It was as if at that moment, every ancestor of the Towry family had been awakened to the birth of a new descendent.

I clutched the baby closer to my chest and searched the darkened hallway for any sign of J.B. Towry.

"Hurry," Terran said. "Let me help you down the stairs."

"The keys to the car are in the sitting room," I said.

The whispers grew around us. "What is that?" Terran said.

"You can hear them?"

"Yes, it's like someone's in my head."

I cringed. "It's him. He's trying to work his way into your thoughts."

Terran pressed on his temples with the heels of his hands. "It's horrible." He doubled over for a moment then stood with a strained look in his eye. "The sounds are like nails clawing down a chalkboard."

"Don't let him in," I said, shuffling faster through the corridors toward the sitting room and dragging Terran along behind me.

As we turned the corner and entered the sitting room, a cold pit of fear sank into my core. I stopped and backed up to the wall.

Sitting next to the fireplace was the skeletal figure of J.B. Towry. His demented eyes turned toward me.

"What the hell is that?" Terran said.

"J.B. Towry. He's come for the baby."

Terran turned me to face him. "We have to run. We'll run for the road."

"I can't run. I can't get far in the night."

His eyes searched mine. "I'll stay then. You go."

"No way. I won't leave you."

The baby cried.

"It's our only chance," Terran said. "Let him try to get into my thoughts. I'll fight him as long as I can. You go. Get past the gate. Don't look back."

I shook my head.

Before we could say another word to each other Terran pressed on his temples again and screamed in pain. A moment later, his eyes rolled back into his head.

I stepped away from him and looked back to the chair beside the fire. The ghostly image of J.B. Towry was gone. When I looked to Terran I screamed. "No, please. No!"

Terran caught me and ripped the baby from my arms, unraveling the blanket to hold the naked infant. He held up the baby with two hands to examine it.

My baby screamed.

I pressed my fist to my mouth. Tears flooded my eyes. "You can't. You can't!"

I thought right there I'd see my baby's neck twisted and his little form flop helplessly to the ground. I pounded my fists against his chest, but Terran shoved me to the ground and before I knew it, he had moved toward the back door and out into the night. I knew he'd throw the baby into Willow Creek like he'd done with the others or into a field to watch it suffer. He would laugh and take pleasure as the baby screamed and writhed beneath the full moon to its death.

I wouldn't let that happen. I rushed toward the fireplace and threw the screen to the side.

In the distance, the baby cried. I looked out the window. Terran was walking toward the dock. The rippling black water like obsidian in the distance was ready to take my child to its eternal underwater grave.

I flung myself into the hearth. I shifted the grate aside and pulled open the ash trap. Beneath the ground, I stretched my arm and felt for the top of the metal box. It was still there. I pulled it out and flung open the lid.

My eyes widened. My breath hitched in my chest as I stared at the black heart of J.B. Towry beating rapidly. How it did so, I couldn't explain. I only knew that it had pulsed like this for over one hundred years, the true heart of Whitehall Manor.

I picked it up feeling its power in my hands. I had to destroy it. But there wasn't time to start a fire. The baby screamed again. I pulled myself up and rushed outside into the darkness to chase after them.

Near the water's edge, at the end of the dock, Terran stood holding my screaming child. He raised it into the air. The night was black except for the moon. I shuddered to a stop. All he had to do was let go.

"No!" I screamed as I held up J.B. Towry's heart, squeezing it tight in my clenched fist.

Terran turned to face me.

"If you kill my child," I yelled. "I will destroy you. I will ensure that your reign of terror ends tonight. I will make sure what's left of you burns for eternity in the pits of hell."

CHAPTER
TWENTY-NINE

Terran's eyes were aglow in the dark but his face had contorted to the shape of J.B. Towry's.

I inched closer. The black heart beat faster in my hands. The baby's screams had softened to whimpers. I only hoped it wasn't too late and my child hadn't been harmed. I made my way to the edge of the dock so that now I was standing beside the monster that had taken over Terran's body.

"Give me my baby," I demanded.

J.B. Towry smiled. That wicked and crooked grin told me he enjoyed seeing the suffering in my eyes. "You've found the heart of Whitehall Manor," he said.

"I don't know how you did this. I don't know how you were able to manipulate your death or convince others to act out your madness, but what I do know is that this ends tonight."

"You end tonight," he said. "Once you and this baby are gone, there can be no others. I've already looked into the future. Your child will drown in Willow Creek. You will follow."

"I won't let you kill him." I reached for the baby, but Terran stepped away and lifted my infant son by his ankles over the water. I fought against tears and an internal scream that lodged in my throat.

Before I could say another word, a voice from somewhere near the house yelled out, "Stop right there!"

I turned to see Detective Richards. His gun was raised and pointed at Terran.

"No!" I yelled to him. "Don't shoot."

As the detective came closer, the ghost narrowed its fixed glare at me.

The baby screamed. His echoes bounced off the water so loud I was sure it could be heard miles downstream.

Then, my newborn son slipped from Terran's fingers and I dropped the black heart. It splashed into the water below as I lunged.

A moment later, gunfire rang out.

Terran crumpled onto the dock just as I caught our child in my hands, nearly tumbling into the water. I steadied myself and clutched his soft body to my chest, kissing his cheeks and sobbing.

When I turned to look at Terran, his eyes had returned to dark blue.

The outline of J.B. Towry's face had vanished. I kneeled at his side and kissed his cheeks. "Please, don't leave me," I whispered.

He held my hand and with one finger stroked the baby's cheek. "Christopher," he whispered.

"Yes," I said. "Our child's name is Christopher."

He gripped my hand and with the last of his breath said, "Don't let him win." Then Terran's eyes began to glaze over. Beneath the moonlight, his skin paled.

The ache inside of me was too much to bear. My gaze

drifted down to the hole in his shirt. I pushed it up to see the wound in his chest near his heart.

"No," I moaned. Tears surfaced as I rocked to my heels.

Detective Richards came to my side and took the baby from me.

I looked at Terran. His eyes were fixed on the moon. I breathed out and buried my face on his chest, sobbing, "I love you."

"Come on, Anne," the detective said, trying to pull me up. "Let's get you out of here."

"It's not his fault," I said, twisting away. "You killed an innocent man."

"He's gone," the detective said.

It took a minute to understand that I was going to walk away from this evening with my child and my life, but what I had to sacrifice to have it was unbearable.

I listened for a moment for J.B. Towry's voice. There was nothing around me. Not a whisper, threat, or curse. The warm summer air swept through my hair. The night was silent except for the whimpering of my baby. My child, Christopher Towry.

When I slowly stood, I searched the dark water off the end of the dock where the black beating heart had fallen. The still water reflected back my twisted image.

Then suddenly, J.B. Towry's voice pressed into my ear. "You will not stop me."

There was no time to waste. I dove into Willow Creek. A terrible ache pulsed throughout my body despite the water's warmth. My head tingled and I thought in that moment that J.B. Towry had been right. I would drown in the water. My baby would follow.

I kicked to the bottom of Willow Creek to the soft sandy floor. In the dark, I searched for the heart knowing it was an impossible task. How could I possibly have thought I could find something as dark as the heart in an even darker world?

My lungs tightened. I grasped again feeling shells and slime between my fingers. A sharp rock cut my hand. Again, my mind began to scream for air. I couldn't give in. I couldn't let J.B. Towry win.

Turning myself around, I kicked against the piling when suddenly without touching anything, I extended my arms and felt the vibrations before me. The pulsing heart beat out a rhythm that promised its survival. It whispered it would go on. The dark vibrations transmitted echoes of the past. I visualized great evil.

With the last seconds of air left in my lungs, I swam closer allowing the pulsations to grow until I thought I could no longer bear it. My father's face appeared before me, and then Seraphine's. A moment later, I saw Caroline, her agonizingly forlorn face and crystal white hair illuminated the darkness. Below me the heart stood out beating on the creek floor. I reached for it. The tips of my fingers brushed against it. I grabbed it and the rock that had cut me then kicked to the surface, swimming back toward the dock.

I rushed to climb up the ladder, moaning in pain with each step as I felt my muscles contract. My soaked robe clung to my skin. The dock was empty except for Terran's body. Trickles of his blood dripped between the planks into the water. I put the heart down.

Detective Richards now stood on the grass far enough away that I couldn't see his eyes, but knew by the way he twisted and held his temples he was fighting the possession.

There were but seconds before J.B. Towry would have

full control of the detective. Baby Christopher wailed. My pulse soared as I began to run toward him but then stopped.

The detective held up a hand as if to say it wasn't safe. He screamed and hit his head with his fists.

"Fight it!" I yelled.

The detective's eyes shifted and I knew it was J.B. Towry's gaze that bore into me.

Even from afar, it felt as if he was beside me. Only now the ghost saw that his heart lay on the end of the dock and the rock that had cut me only moments before was gripped firmly in my right hand.

I wasted no time. I spun back to the heart and kneeled before it.

The detective yelled and ran down the dock toward me.

Raising my arm, I brought down the rock hard on the black heart.

The first hit stopped it from beating.

The detective crumbled to his knees.

The second hit cut into it. Black blood oozed from its core.

J.B. Towry's face morphed inside of the detective's skull. The pained look told me what I was doing was working.

I smashed the heart again. It tore clear in two.

Detective Richards fell to his side as the ghost of J.B. Towry rose in a dark shadow from him. Finally, I could see the ghost's torment. The apparition tore at itself and twisted in its last moments of agony.

I smashed the pieces of the heart again, damning his soul to hell as I did so.

J.B. Towry's piercing scream echoed around me.

I dropped the rock and pressed my hands to my ears until the screeching sound thinned to a whistle that went on for several seconds causing the birds from a nearby tree to fly into the moonlight.

Red-tailed hawks. A cluster of them flew scattered into the night. A few moments later, the noise faded to static and was gone.

Silence surrounded me then slowly the sounds of the world returned.

Below me, the pulsating organ dulled to gray. Its pieces disintegrated to ash and slipped into the water below. Some of it carried away in the wind.

I forced myself up, aching terribly as I limped toward Christopher who whimpered in the grass.

"Anne?" The detective's hand gripped my ankle.

I glanced down to see his bright green eyes restored.

"What happened?" he asked.

"You'll be okay," I said to him as he let go of me and began to sit up.

At the end of the dock, I picked up Christopher and held him tight to my chest. "No one will ever hurt you now." I kissed his cheeks and forehead. "The curse is over."

CHAPTER
THIRTY

The long night of questions took its toll on me. I had been seen by Dr. McCallister in the hospital and the next day I was arrested on suspicion of murder, Penelope's murder. I sat again in the interrogation room. Christopher, born one month too soon, stayed in the hospital.

The investigator, a burly and aggressive man named Flynn who was brought in from a neighboring town, narrowed his gaze at me as he demanded I retell the story one more time.

"When will I be able to see Christopher?" I asked.

"That's up to the judge to decide," he said.

"I can't see my child?"

"We don't know if you're a threat to your child."

I turned my seat to face Detective Richards who stood in the corner quietly observing. "You saw what happened. How can you accuse me of not trying to defend my child?"

"Let's leave him out of this," Flynn said.

"He was there," I said. "He knows what happened."

Flynn glanced to Detective Richards. "Are you going to

tell me she's telling the truth? There was a ghost who possessed her boyfriend and you?"

Detective Richards stayed quiet. After a moment, he said, "I heard Anne scream. I rushed from my car around the house to where I saw them standing at the end of the dock. You know the rest. I've already given my statement."

The investigator smiled. "That's right. Detective Richards saw your fiancée threatening to drop Christopher into Willow Creek. Terran was going to drown your child and yet you still defend him. You know what that tells me? It tells me you wanted your child dead."

"No, I didn't," I said, slamming my fist on the table.

"What about your housekeeper? Did you kill her because she was having an affair with Terran?"

"No."

"How did she fall from the window?"

"I told you."

"I'm not buying the possession story, Anne. Give us another one."

"It's the truth. Even if you don't believe me, it doesn't matter. I didn't push her during the struggle. I was giving birth. She rushed toward Terran. He only backed away from the window. She accidentally fell to her death."

"Maybe you set Terran up to fight her."

"I didn't."

For the next hour, I retold my story to the investigator while Detective Richards said nothing and then finally left the room, leaving me to fend for myself.

I told them everything in the hope that they'd reunite me with baby Christopher. The black heart of J.B. Towry was smashed to bits. It no longer pulsated its energy through every room of Whitehall Manor. J.B. Towry no longer had control of the home. The curse had ended.

J.B. Towry had taken nearly everything from me. Terran lay dead on a stone-cold slab in the mortuary. A single bullet hole had pierced his chest, killing him only moments after. Penelope lay nearby in the same room, on a different slab, an autopsy in effect as they examined the exact cause of her death. Her neck twisted and eyes fixed. It wouldn't take long to figure that out. I was sure I would pass out from exhaustion. My breasts ached and I needed my child.

"Please let me see Christopher," I begged the investigator once more.

"What were you and Terran going to do to your child?" he asked.

"Nothing. I was trying to save my baby."

"There were reports of screaming all night coming from Whitehall Manor. Your screams and the baby's. The screams echoed downstream so loud that people sitting on their porches called emergency services."

The woman with soft lines around her eyes who had sat quietly and patiently listening to my retelling of the story eventually explained her role in all of this. "I'm the head of the psychiatric unit at Baltimore's Health Center."

A tremor worked its way into my hand as I pressed it to my chest. "No. I'm not crazy."

"We don't like to use that word," she said, slowly standing and coming to my side. "I think what would be best for you and the baby is to have a little rest."

"A rest? No."

She nodded and smiled.

The investigator stood and shook his head. "It's always something with you Towrys, isn't it?" He walked to the door with the woman. I could hear them. They were talking about the paperwork, the judge's order, the ambulance that would be coming for me, the length of time I would need under observation, and the best treatment for someone suffering from my condition.

Tears flooded my eyes as I stood but it was too late.

They left the room. The door clanged shut.

I eased back to my chair and sat. There was little chance of returning to Whitehall Manor tonight but I knew I would. Even if I stayed in the psychiatric unit for days, weeks, or months, I knew I would eventually find my way back home and once again resume my role as the lady of the manor. I twisted my hands as I ached for my baby. As I stood and paced the room, a thought came to me.

What the investigator and the woman from the psychiatric unit didn't know was that whatever lay in my future hardly matched what I had just come through. I had survived a generations old curse. I had changed the course of the future for myself and Christopher. I took my seat and waited for their return knowing there was something to look forward to. It was the end of the summer and soon a new season would usher in change.

I pondered what the Marigold Garden must look like at this moment. The flowering must have slowed with the heat of the summer but that could be fixed. I would hire new gardeners and they would deadhead the spent blossoms or I would do it myself. I smiled knowing with the changing season and cooler weather the blooms would return to their pristine majesty. Their pungent scent would carry with it the promise of souls returning from the dead. Seraphine, Salazar, and Terran would follow the trail back to Whitehall Manor, and baby Christopher and I would be there awaiting their return.

AUTHOR'S NOTE

Thank you for reading.
If you enjoyed *The Curse of Whitehall Manor,* please consider
leaving a review on Amazon or Goodreads.

WANT MORE?

Anne Towry finds herself locked in an asylum fighting to prove her sanity and desperate to return to her newborn child and Whitehall Manor.

With a new and unexpected relative coming to her rescue, will Anne finally find peace or will she be yet another victim to the Towry curse?

Find out what happens next in Book 3,

The Fall of Whitehall Manor.

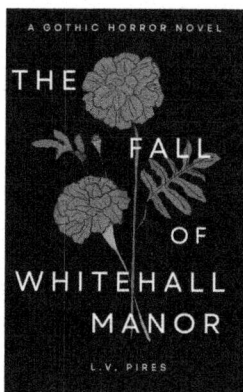

ABOUT THE AUTHOR

L.V. Pires is the best-selling author of horror fiction, including THE WAITING MORTUARY, VIGIL BLACK, AND DEATH WATCH.

To find out more about upcoming releases, join the L.V. Pires newsletter at lisavpires.com

ALSO BY L.V. PIRES

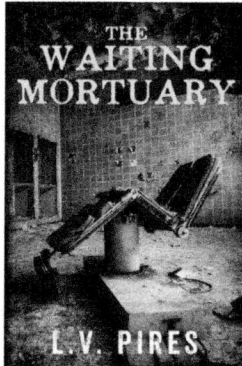

The Waiting Mortuary

Welcome to *The Waiting Mortuary* where embalming is free whether you're dead or alive.

Bash Trawler wants to find an easy summer job. When he discovers an advertisement in the local paper for night watch at a nearby funeral home he jumps at the chance to make quick money. But staying up all night watching corpses for an eccentric war vet turns into something out of his worst nightmares.

Casey McClair wants to make the tennis team. Popularity has never come easily to her and she's willing to practice into the late evening and follow all the rules of the game if it means she'll finally find acceptance. But when she's kidnapped, she'll have to fight to survive a harrowing ordeal with a cold and calculated serial killer.

Serial Killer X knows about pain. He's been through the worst of what humans do to each other. The thrill is in the fight and he'll make sure his victims know it.

Three stories intertwine to tell the sickening tale of what goes on inside **THE WAITING MORTUARY.**

What readers are saying:

★★★★★ "Sick, twisted, thrilling, engrossing. I was unable to put it down! I loved it...especially the twist at the end!"

★★★★★ "The Waiting Mortuary has a lot of twists & turns & just when you think it's over...it grabs you again."

★★★★★ "My heart was racing for the entire last half of the book and it still didn't slow down for quite a while after I finished."

★★★★★ "All 3 characters are brought together with their own stories to tell in this intriguing book. It all comes together in a fast-paced story."

★★★★★ "One of my new favorites. Tense and well-paced, it's definitely something I would suggest to others."

Vigil Black

She fought off a serial killer but will she be strong enough to fight the evil she brought back?

It's been three months since Casey survived a harrowing ordeal with a cold-blooded serial killer. No one expected her to bounce back right away, but Casey's agonizing recovery is riddled with more than trauma. She should be getting on with her life, returning to school, enjoying parties, and maybe even kindling a new romance, but none of that is possible when she's tortured by the memories of what happened inside the waiting mortuary.

With a series of blackouts threatening to destroy her and a new predator murdering people she knows, Casey begins to question her reality and decides to return to the waiting mortuary to find out the truth of who she really is and the evil she may have brought back from last summer.

Caught in a maze of what's real and imagined, Casey will be forced to pull apart everything she knows to uncover who she can trust and who is behind a new string of murders that have hit Westport.

Can Casey defeat her inner demons to discover the truth? Or will what she finds destroy her?

∽

Don't miss **VIGIL BLACK,** the second book of *The Waiting Mortuary* series by L.V. Pires. If you like Darcy Coates, Jeremy Bates, or Jeff Strand then this horror novel will have you turning the pages!

What readers are saying:

★★★★★ **"Completely terrifying!"**

★★★★★ **"A total mind warp!"**

★★★★★ **"Once again L.V. Pires rocks the ending."**

★★★★★ **"The waiting mortuary keeps getting scarier."**

★★★★★ **"The story gave me chills."**

★★★★★ **"I can't wait to read Book 3!"**

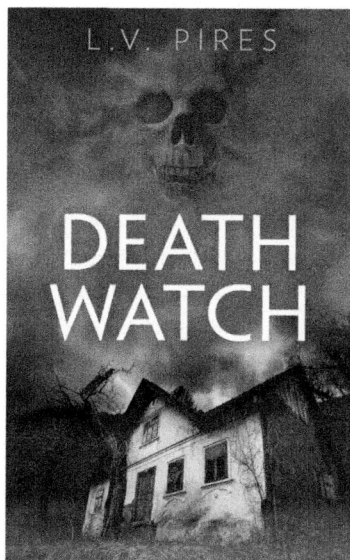

Death Watch

It's been a long time since Jack Skilton wrote an article for *The Westport Press*, but when rumors of a sinister presence lurking inside the waiting mortuary begin to spread, he's sent to Kessler's Funeral Home to investigate a possible haunting and what he discovers will definitely make front-page news if only he can live long enough to write about it.

Find out what happens in this horror thriller with supernatural elements written for audiences who enjoy turning pages at breakneck speed. Be warned this story is not for the faint of heart. What begins as a mystery will evolve into total terror.

Don't miss DEATH WATCH, the third book in *The Waiting Mortuary* series by L.V. Pires.

Although in a series, this novel can also **STAND ALONE**.